PRAISE FOR THE SPANISH LANGUAGE EDITION

"Isaac Goldemberg's first detective novel is a vertiginous, parodic, efficacious work; it gathers together all the stereotypes of the genre and honors its predecessors, both in literature and film. In a very brief space in time and very quickly, thanks to its memorable cocaine addict protagonist—as Robert de Niro in Sergio Leone's film—we learn that love is sweet and miserable as in the sentimental boleros and waltzes. And that dreams are actually prophecies, because from the first line of the novel we are warned: 'the coming events had begun to cast their shadow.'"

—Margo Glantz (International Award Sor Juana Inés de la Cruz and FIL Guadalajara Prize 2010)

"This new novel by Isaac Goldemberg marks the return of a great Latin American novelist, the same one that drew the attention of critics and the public with novels like *The Fragmented Life of Don Jacobo Lerner*, *Play by Play* and *The Name of the Father*. Now, in the juicy and fascinating plot of *Remember the Scorpion* we see shine, once again, the imagination and firm prose of this great Peruvian writer."

—Mempo Giardinelli (Rómulo Gallegos International Novel Prize and National Book Award in Mexico)

T0131369

"*Remember the Scorpion* is a true *genre noir* novel since we are not faced with the analytical police drama in which gifted detectives are able to solve, effortlessly and perfectly, the most enigmatic cases; instead we are confronted by a story that plunges us into the murkiness of the human heart and also shows us how the corrupt economic wheels (mixed with the political ones) get in the way, and even impede the pursuit of justice. In the last few decades, many detective novels have been written in Peru and Latin America; but few possess the artistic quality and depth of *Remember the Scorpion*." (*El Comercio*, **Lima**)

"*Remember the Scorpion* has been written with acuity and a full understanding of our reality, with a touch of dry humor and fully utilizing an arsenal of subtle seductive tactics... However, no matter how sordid and dark the events, Isaac Goldemberg doesn't forget about love, which surfaces, rises and leaves its mark on many parts of the story with a sweet tenderness and a whiff of surreptitious melodrama, derived from the disenchantment of the lovers once they learn that their feelings are always subject to the ironic paradoxes of destiny." (*Noticias del Interior*, **Lima**)

"*Remember the Scorpion*, Isaac Goldemberg's extraordinary and most recent novel, has forced me to ponder the concept of dystopia, or cacotopia, as a means of understanding the literature, the government and the armed forces of Peru and Latin America, as well as the misery and growing extreme violence which is customary in Third World countries... In Goldemberg's novel, we experience an intertwining of a cinematic virtual reality which is absorbing and passionate from beginning to end... *Remember the Scorpion* is not merely a detective novel." (*Raíces*, **Madrid**)

REMEMBER THE
SCORPION

A NOVEL

ISAAC GOLDEMBERG

TRANSLATED FROM THE SPANISH BY
JONATHAN TITTLER

WITH AN INTRODUCTION BY
SAÚL SOSNOWSKI

THE UNNAMED PRESS
LOS ANGELES, CA

The Unnamed Press
1551 Colorado Blvd., Suite #201
Los Angeles, CA 90041

www.unnamedpress.com

First published in North America by The Unnamed Press

1 3 5 7 9 10 8 6 4 2

Copyright 2015 © Isaac Goldemberg
Translation copyright 2015 © Jonathan Tittler

ISBN: 978-1-939419-19-4
Library of Congress Control Number: 2014948168

This book is distributed by Publishers Group West

Printed in the United States of America

Designed by Scott Arany

CONTENTS

BRIDGING IDENTITIES

A BRIEF INTRODUCTION
TO ISAAC GOLDEMBERG

ISAAC GOLDEMBERG, a longtime resident of New York City, is an internationally recognized and award-winning writer and poet. In 1976 he published *The Fragmented Life of Don Jacobo Lerner*—a classic among major Latin American novels which has gone through several editions in Spanish, French, English and Hebrew, and which in 2001 was selected by an international panel of critics—convened by the Yiddish Book Center—as one of the 100 greatest Jewish books of the past 150 years. *Play by Play* and *El nombre del padre*, two other novels, are available in Spanish, French, and Italian. He has also published several books of poetry: *Hombre de paso (Just Passing Through)*, *Los autorretratos y las máscaras (Self-Portraits and Masks)*, *Peruvian blues*, which received

1

the Peruvian PEN Club Poetry Award for 2001, *Libro de las transformaciones*, and *Diálogos conmigo y mis otros*, among others. He is also the author of two plays: *Hotel AmériKKa* (published in Spanish and English), and *Golpe de gracia*, for which he received the prestigious Premio Estival de Teatro 2003.

When reflecting on issues of identity in twentieth-century Peruvian literature, José María Arguedas (1911–1969) and Isaac Goldemberg come to mind. Arguedas addressed head-on the uneasy linkages between European and local indigenous cultures; Goldemberg has added Jewish traditions to that already conflictive relationship. Although in both his prose and his poetry, he mingles the sounds of the "shofar" and the "quena," a middle ground remains as elusive as any attempt to articulate in unison both Spanish and Quechua as conveyors of radically different views of the world.

The encounter of cultures has never been peaceful, except when the conquered relinquished their own selves to a vision imposed by others. Co-existence has always been problematic (and still bloody in too many quarters) when claims are made to possessing the sole truth. Even a purported solution cedes to either a dominant culture or caves in to a powerful and growing minority. Other than outright conflict, negotiations between competing forces generate the potential for significant literary prowess. That was true in the most dramatic texts written by Arguedas; it is also true, albeit in a different vein, in Goldemberg's works.

If one were to seek out the axis around which Goldemberg's literature revolves, "identity" undoubtedly emerges above every other motif. From *The Fragmented Life of Don Jacobo Lerner*, to his most recent collection of poetry *Diálogos conmigo y mis otros* (2013) and this, his latest novel *Remember the Scorpion*, Goldemberg reflects on the core issue that shapes him as a multicultural writer (and persona). We are not dealing simply with hybrid cultures, and not solely with the often-studied complexities of mestizaje. His multi-layered works bring together Eastern European (Ashkenazi) Jewry and Judaism; indigenous practices that surge forth from Catholicism as performed by Peruvian "mestizos;" contemporary predicaments and Colonial legacies; the unraveling of a familial Peruvian setting and a potential reconstruction in a New York habitat; the linguistic mix of Spanish-Hebrew-Quechua and linguistic variations of English and Spanglish. The sum of all these ingredients, and a folk version of both Judaism and Christianity, are wrapped together in a body that cannot be contained nor signified by any one of the boxes so cherished by pollsters and census analysts. What is striking, moreover, is that multiple identities are oftentimes presented through the humorous vein that is a trademark of many masters of nineteenth and twentieth-century Yiddish literature.

Rather than engage in the futile game of influences and predecessors, it seems more useful to anticipate that those who come to Goldemberg's pages from the Hispanic tradition will probably move towards the Inca Garcilaso de la Vega and, as I myself did at the beginning, to Arguedas. Those steeped in U.S. letters will recognize traces that range from Bellow to Roth. Yiddish speakers will recognize a touch of Scholem Aleichem and Bashevis Singer. Even Woody Allen is not too far off when crossing a New York street, although it is the Nuyorican poets who are more likely to recognize a kindred spirit in Goldemberg's search for a word that enunciates multiple identities and (be)longings.

Goldemberg's signature is traced across fragmented and overlapping identities. These are not shifting identities; at most, readers will find varying degrees of emphases as he attempts to balance the motifs that inform his literary pages. It is not surprising, therefore, that in his case we may speak of the "aesthetics of fragmentation" and, at the same time, ponder the "aesthetics of integration."

Identity is a springboard for analyzing Jewish-Latin American traditions, as well as considering literature on the margins of the Latin American canon (and for some to also ponder their own place in the universe). One of the most telling statements on the significance of Goldemberg's production is precisely his place in contemporary literature. Plainly stated: it is inconceivable not to include at least one of his works when addressing Latin American-Jewish letters. Furthermore, it would be folly to navigate Peruvian letters without including an author who, from a unique vantage point, raises questions about the very definition of nationality and goes to the very core of "mestizaje."

Goldemberg's characters may lead us to wonder whether he privileges the existence of a "Universal Jew," of someone able to become acclimated to any culture while maintaining some version of "being Jewish." Both his fiction and his most poignant poetry incorporate this problematic dimension. Conversely (pun not necessarily intended), they also challenge all conventional definitions of "Latin American" as inextricably linked to a dominant culture and a majority religion. To date, his works posit shifting and uneasy movements within multiple identities, not the dissolution of any of them.

Goldemberg's texts affirm that fragmentary / fragmented beings can indeed be whole. That is how they stay with us, as they also elicit our own pursuit of what multiple identities signify. Perhaps, therein lies the very core of Goldemberg's aesthetics.

Saúl Sosnowski
Professor, Latin American Literature
University of Maryland, College Park
Editor, *Hispamérica*

REMEMBER THE
SCORPION

To my wife

Time is the best author:
It always finds a perfect ending.
Charles Chaplin

This afternoon in Lima it's raining.
[...]
This afternoon it's raining, raining hard. And I
Don't feel like living, my heart!
César Vallejo

Love is the trap you set for men in order to drape
yourself in their shivers, to feed on their tears.
Edmond Jabès

LIMA, JUNE 1970

TUESDAY, THE 2ND

NOT SUSPECTING THAT future events had already begun to cast their shadow, Captain Simón Weiss drove his car along the almost deserted streets of downtown Lima, avoiding the rubble caused by the earthquake that two days earlier had devastated the city and a good part of the northern region of the country. He was heading toward Central Police HQ, summoned by Inspector Cato Castro Castro, better known as The Fox, a famous cop who in the 1950s had been instrumental in the capture of widely feared criminals like Tatán and The Flash, so nicknamed because of the speed with which she committed her break-ins.

A radio announcer's voice filled the car:

"...The earthquake has left the country mired in chaos. The entire city of Yungay has been buried. In Huaraz the destruction is almost total..."

Weiss changed stations:

"...The number of victims is estimated at eighty thousand. The President of the Republic, General Juan Velasco Alvarado, has urged the population to remain calm and promised immediate assistance from the Armed Forces and other branches of the..."

He changed stations again.

"...fifteen minutes into the first half and Peru is trailing Bulgaria, one–zero. The Peruvian team looks totally demoralized, the full weight of the nation's tragedy on its shoulders."

Exasperated, the captain clicked off the radio just as he pulled in front of HQ. Two policemen carrying machine guns guarded the entrance. From the inside pocket of his overcoat Weiss extracted a little plastic bag, opened it, brought it to his nose, and sniffed in the white powder. He then replaced the bag in the pocket, wiped his nostrils while looking at himself in the rearview mirror, and got out of the car.

An ambulance sped past him. Not bothering to turn and look at it, he stopped an instant, disturbed by the siren's howling. Then he resumed walking toward the building. His step was fast, nervous.

As soon as he crossed the threshold of the entrance the policeman on duty gave him a military salute. Weiss returned the salute, set off down a hallway, and came to a door with a nameplate:

Inspector Cato Castro Castro
Director / Homicide Division

Weiss rapped his knuckles on the door.

"Come in!" the inspector shouted.

Weiss entered, giving his habitual quick and casual military salute. The inspector, buried amongst the heaps of papers that covered his desk, did not look up. Behind him, next to the wall, on two golden poles, were the Peruvian flag and that of the Police Force, and a photograph of General Juan Velasco Alvarado, who glared across the room with penetrating eyes.

"Inspector, sorry I'm late, but..."

"Yeah, yeah, the city's a mess. Five hundred dead in Lima and two hundred in the downtown area alone! You two know each other, right? Captain Weiss... Lieutenant Kanashiro."

Weiss turned and his eyes met those of the lieutenant, who saluted him with a ceremonious bow. Weiss returned the gesture with an irritated nod of the head and flopped into an armchair before the inspector's desk, rubbing his eyes. They had dark pouches under them, and he looked haggard.

"You don't look so hot, Captain," the inspector pointed out helpfully.

"Not enough sleep," Weiss hoisted himself out of the chair and went to the window. Something had caught his attention. Through the glass he could see part of the avenue covered with adobe and brick fragments. Across the street, atop the roof of a church, two bald turkey vultures with ash-colored feathers fought over the remains of a rat. "Every night I've had the same dream. It's killing my sleep," he added.

"Now what could you be dreaming about?" the inspector said, outlining an almost malicious smile, full of mischief.

"A scorpion," Weiss muttered.

"A scorpion?"

"An old man and a scorpion. But we're not here to talk about that," Weiss said, returning to the armchair, sinking into the depths of a vague memory.

The inspector got up from his seat.

"Well, we've got a fairly gruesome case on our hands," he said. "A few hours ago, firefighters discovered the body of a Japanese man at the Shima Pool Hall. The dead man is the owner. I want you to take up the case, with Kanashiro as your second."

Weiss stood up. He took a few steps toward the inspector.

"I know you like to work alone, Captain, but this is a special case," preempted the inspector. "The lieutenant here speaks Japanese and knows the Japanese community from the inside. Besides, he's an ex-cadet from the Leoncio Prado Military Academy, like you. I hear that in itself constitutes a bond."

"It will be a great honor to work under your command,

Captain," interjected the young lieutenant.

Weiss took the measure of his new partner in a glance. "OK," he concluded.

"I am most grateful, Captain," Kanashiro said with another bow.

"Then go!" ordered the inspector, adding crabbily, "Come on now, you're losing precious time!"

Kanashiro opened the door with a respectful flourish and stood aside for the captain. In the hallway leading to the technician's room boomed the voice of Captain Aránguiz.

"Hey, Sherlock!"

Weiss did not take the bait. He kept on walking, accompanied by Kanashiro. Impeccably dressed, with brilliantine in both his hair and his expression, Aránguiz caught up with them and grabbed Weiss's arm as they neared the exit.

"So they stuck you with Kanashiro. What, don't you have any friends in the government anymore?" mocked Aránguiz.

Weiss broke loose of Aránguiz and kept on walking, unflappable.

"Don't forget, Sherlock: I'm here if you need me!" shouted Aránguiz after them.

"He's envious, Captain," the lieutenant observed softly, when they were out of ear-shot.

"Since when do you read people's thoughts, Lieutenant?" shot back Weiss.

"Not thoughts, Captain. Emotions. Emotions are as recognizable as uniforms."

"I don't like a smart-ass," growled Weiss, and Kanashiro shut his mouth.

Their feet echoed through the hallway. The station had emptied out into the city, to handle various aspects of the disaster, and this deserted quiet seemed to embolden the lieutenant to try again: "Detective work is an art, and only those with the soul of an artist can be any good at it."

Weiss stopped, fixing his eyes on the lieutenant.

"You said that," added Kanashiro.

"I said that?"

"Yes, when you visited the academy to talk to us about becoming a policeman, remember? I knew I wanted to be a policeman, but after listening to you, I knew I would become a detective.

"Detective work is an art, and only those with the soul of an artist can be any good at it," muttered Weiss under his breath. He laughed cynically, then swiveled on his heel and swung open the door to the technician's room. Inside, a few men huddled around a small television, the match between Peru and Bulgaria playing itself out in miniature. They went straight up to Huamani, the photographer, and Bocanegra, the fingerprint specialist.

Weiss signaled to the men and they stepped away from the TV.

"Get your gear," he told them. "Meet us at the Shima

Pool Hall, corner of Tacna and Superunda."

"But Captain, the second half just started," complained Huamani.

"Have a heart, Captain," Bocanegra seconded him.

"No problem with me, boys," said Weiss. "Go tell The Fox you need a little extra time before you help us investigate a murder. Go ahead."

Grumbling, Huamani and Bocanegra went to gather their gear and Weiss pulled out his pack of cigarettes. He offered one to Kanashiro, who declined. Weiss lit up. Both men went over to the television set. The Peruvian players were in possession of the ball. The screen said: BULGARIA 1, PERU 0.

"One-zero... We need a miracle," said Kanashiro.

"Don't worry," said Weiss. "We've got this match in the bag. It's in the stars."

The captain blew a mouthful of smoke at the screen and turned quickly toward the exit, followed by the lieutenant.

———————

When Weiss and Kanashiro reached the pool hall, Huamani and Bocanega were already posted there, waiting for them in the entryway that faced Avenida Tacna. The other doorway, laid waste by the earthquake, looked out on Conde de Superunda Street. Uniformed police guarded both entrances. On Avenida Tacna, flames and smoke swirled around a three-story mansion that had collapsed, flipping over horizontally, stranding several people amidst its rubble. A squad of fire fighters bravely battled the flames, and another one stirred up the debris in search of possible survivors. On the other side of the avenue, part of the arcade in the Church of Santa Rosa's atrium had collapsed. The bridge that joined Tacna with the Rímac District had broken away slightly, and on the other side of the river the hills had disappeared behind the smoke.

On Conde de Superunda Street several adobe houses had fallen off their foundations. Across from the pool hall, in a bar filled with men and women in an almost catatonic state, with terror etched on their faces, an enormous television screen showed the second half of the Peru-Bulgaria match. The Peruvian team was now trailing two to one.

Weiss and his men were about to enter the pool hall when a slight earth tremor struck, threatening broader havoc. The people who were in the dive poured out into the street and ran toward the church, piling up in the atrium. Fear kept them from breathing. The aftershock lasted a couple of seconds, and as soon as the earth stopped shaking, they ran back into the joint to continue watching the match.

Recovered from the tremor, Weiss and his men entered the pool hall. Part of the roof had caved in. Stout beams, adobe bricks, and ceramic shingles lay strewn over the clay tile floor. The left-hand wall, decorated with Japanese landscapes drawn with soft colors and fine strokes, showed deep cracks. A gigantic photo of an atomic explosion, retouched in bright colors, covered half the wall on the right. The mushroom cloud rose above an ashen sky. Its center was pure turbulence, a gray-purple mass with a red core, and its base looked like a dense fog. Below that scene was a city enveloped in flames, with smoke rising from an enormous bed of embers. The other half of the wall bore another photo, showing an enormous surface of scorched earth over which remained standing a solitary arch in the form of a pagoda, its roof and columns charred.

Hypnotized by the explosion and the total destruction caused by the bomb, Weiss and Kanashiro stood there transfixed, with their eyes glued to the photographs. They were snapped out of their trance by a policeman who, after saluting them, led them to the back of the main hall. Some twenty tables stretched to the bar, forming two rows. Behind the counter, on top of a shelf, there was a TV set. Above the bar, bleachers had been erected, from which the clientele of the pool hall could witness the tournaments that were held monthly. The best pool players in Lima attended those tournaments, including Adolfo Suárez, who a few years previous had been crowned triple world pool champion in Amsterdam.

Weiss and his men went over to the table, where they found the victim's body. It was lying on its back, hands and legs nailed to the wood, and in each one of its hands, as if in a holder, reposed a half-spent candle. There were also candles beside its feet. The Japanese man's throat had been slit, and his head dangled back over empty space.

Blood had soaked the once-green cloth of the table, which now wavered between purple and brown. While Weiss and Kanashiro inspected the body, Huamani and Bocanegra got down to work.

"The blood on the neck and floor is fresher than the blood on the table," observed Kanashiro.

"They nailed him to the table first and then slit his throat," said Weiss.

Weiss and Kanashiro went over to the bar. The captain opened the cash register. It was overflowing with bills. A policeman called to them from a landing above the main hall.

"Captain, come see this."

The officer pointed to a hole in the wall, caused by the earthquake, where an old suitcase sat amidst the rubble. Opening it, Weiss found several folders and notebooks. He removed them, and a photo slipped out of one of the folders. He recognized the person in the photograph immediately. It was the deceased—though some twenty-five years younger and wearing the uniform of the Japanese army. Weiss took out another folder from the suitcase and found the victim's ID card.

"Tokayoshi Takashima, native of Hiroshima," he read out loud.

Weiss and Kanashiro looked at each other.

"Hiroshima..." they both said at the same time. Now they understood what those photos were doing on the floor below.

Weiss went on reading:

"Entered Peru in 1945. Peruvian citizen since 1955. Civil status: single."

A great cry erupted outside but Weiss didn't flinch.

"We scored," Kanashiro said quietly, taking the picture from Weiss.

Lost in thought, Weiss cast his eyes all about him as Bocanegra brandished his transistor radio nearby straining to hear details of the score.

Ignoring the fingerprint specialist, Weiss began to quickly rifle through the briefcase, producing another piece of paper, this one with a long scrawl of numbers.

"A combination?" asked the lieutenant.

"There must have been a safe here," said Weiss.

"Not necessarily..." said Kanashiro. Something strange wavered in the lieutenant's voice.

"Maybe that was the motive for the crime," added the captain.

"For money? So why didn't they snatch the contents of the cash register?"

"They weren't after money," said Weiss, moving around the room. "A safe can protect things far more valuable than money."

"In this safe that we don't even know exists."

"Oh, it exists. The question is where has it gone?"

Another collective shout of *goooal* erupted into the pool hall from outside.

"Bocanegra, turn on the TV," ordered the captain.

Bocanegra abandoned his work and ran over to the television behind the bar. A replay of the goal-scoring play appeared on the screen as he snapped it on.

"Oh boy, what a beautiful goal by Nene Cubillas! Peru takes the lead 3–2 and is now on its way to the quarterfinals. Fifteen minutes left in the game!" the announcer yelled.

From the entrance, the reporter Sofía Galindo poked her head in, calling to Kanashiro as a uniformed cop tried to block her from entering. She was a young woman of about twenty-five, pretty, with features more indigenous than European and a confident demeanor that made Weiss uneasy.

"Psst, Kato!" she called with a bright smile.

"Sofía Galindo!" announced Weiss. "How does this girl get to every crime scene nearly as fast as us? Do you know her?"

"She's my fiancée..." stammered the lieutenant.

"This girl, Captain," Galindo said boldly, "Is a crime reporter, and it's a reporter's job..."

"Ahh," Weiss interrupted her, and pointed an accusatory

finger at his new partner, who was turning an unlikely shade of red. "Kanashiro, go handle your girlfriend."

Weiss looked over at Huamani and Bocanegra and gestured for them to follow him to a corner.

"So?" asked Weiss.

"Nothing that catches the eye, Captain," said Bocanegra.

"Any fingerprints?"

"They did a good job of cleaning up after themselves, Captain."

"As soon as the match has ended run the samples over and I mean run," ordered Weiss. And he added, "Huamani, I want the photos first thing in the morning."

"They'll be in your office, Captain."

Huamani and Bocanegra smiled gratefully, and stepped back toward the bar. Suddenly, Sofía Galindo's cameraman appeared in the doorway, aiming his camera at Weiss.

"Back off!" said Weiss, covering his face. "Dammit Kanashiro!"

"Come on, Captain, with that mug, don't you want to be on TV?" The cameraman grinned.

"Do you want me to confiscate the camera?" threatened the captain.

Galindo ran back into the room and intervened, "Jorge, wait for me in the van."

The cameraman obeyed and retreated.

"Tell me, Captain, do you have a theory about the crime yet?" the young reporter pressed as Kanashiro tried to guide her away from the captain and out of the room.

"No theories yet," Weiss yelled, "But I'll be sure to call you when I think of one."

"Well, you can hear mine on tonight's news. Channel Five, at nine. Don't forget."

As Sofía Galindo left, though not before giving Kanashiro a fun-loving wink, two men appeared, escorted by a police officer.

"And who are these two?" asked Weiss.

"My name is Tojishiko Sato, and I am the co-owner of this establishment," answered the younger one. He was well-dressed, arrogant, with a wide stance and broad shoulders.

"And you show up now?"

"I was out of town. I couldn't travel until now, because of the earthquake..."

"And you, who are you?" asked Weiss of the other man. He was a short, bull-like character.

"Akira Fujimoto, in charge of security. He was with me," explained Sato. "Can you tell me what you're doing here?"

"Your partner has been murdered," said Weiss.

"Murdered?"

"Follow me," added the captain.

When they reached the table where the dead man lay, Sato froze, horrified, but Fujimoto appeared to be unmoved.

"They must have killed him to rob the money you kept

in the safe," said Weiss.

"Don't know what you're talking about," replied Sato. Weiss flashed a smile and showed him the paper with the combination written on it. Sato examined it.

"This is news to me," he said. And immediately he asked Fujimoto, in Japanese: "Do you know anything about this?"

Fujimoto shook his head no, shrugging his huge shoulders.

"He doesn't know anything either," Sato explained.

"Of course he doesn't. Who else works in the pool hall?" asked Weiss.

"The cooks, the bartender, the waiters, and the cleaning ladies."

"We'll have to get their statements," said the captain to the lieutenant.

Weiss showed Sato the dead man's photograph.

"What do you know about this?"

"It's the first time I've seen this photo."

"Did your partner have any enemies?" inquired Weiss.

"None that I know of. My partner was a quiet man. The pool hall was practically his whole life. He went out once a week to go to old man Kanashiro's barbershop, the one that's just three blocks from here. They were childhood friends."

The young lieutenant twitched, and quickly looked away.

"That's all for now," Weiss said brusquely. "Leave your address with the lieutenant."

The soccer match was over, and the announcer's effusive voice could barely be heard over the uproarious shouting and foot-stomping of the other policemen. On the television, the Peruvian players hugged each other, celebrating their victory.

"Peru has won! Our boys left their hearts and souls on the field. Today they could not let their fans down, today was a day for miracles!" the announcer's voice resounded inside the murder scene.

Meanwhile, Weiss blasted Kanashiro point-blank.

"So your old man's barber shop is nearby?"

The lieutenant hesitated, then nodded.

Weiss leaned closer, "And you're familiar with Takashima then, too?"

Kanashiro shook his head no, and then both men looked back over to where the crucified man lay on the table.

"You're sure?"

"I'm sure Captain," Kanashiro said emphatically. Then, less so: "But I can talk to my father to see what he can tell us."

Weiss slipped another cigarette into his mouth, "You stay here to wait for the coroner to remove the body. And speak to the neighbors to see what they know. We'll meet tomorrow at the Central Police Headquarters, at ten sharp."

Then Weiss walked out of the building, leaving his anxious lieutenant behind.

He ended up in Chinatown, a few blocks from the Central Market. When he was a block away from the arch that led to Capón Street, the neighborhood's main artery, Weiss felt a thud, in crescendo, that seemed to come from the bowels of the hills. Then, with a great roar, the earth began to sway. The captain made it to the middle of the pavement, and from there, in the brief seconds the aftershock lasted, he saw how the lampposts were shaking, the old trolley rails were twisted, and the adobe-and-straw walls shook as if made of paper. The sidewalks rose and fell in waves, and some dogs ran the length of the streets barking at invisible enemies. Meanwhile, from San Cristóbal Hill, situated a few blocks behind the Plaza de Armas, there descended a cloud of dust that veiled the reddish brilliance of the sun, which, poised to be eclipsed, was suspended above the city sky. Flocks of birds took flight and collided with each other. People poured out into the streets, frightened that their homes might collapse. Men and women dropped to their knees, raising their eyes to heaven and begging God's forgiveness.

No sooner had calm returned than the sky turned dark. Suddenly, a block away, behind the Chinese arch, red lanterns hanging between tall posts lit up, and a group of women wearing white dresses with yellow and red embroidery began to set off skyrockets. They ran up and down the street, chanting spells and tossing amulets to chase away evil spirits and bring good luck.

Weiss reached the Chinese arch, which had miraculously been spared much of the earthquake's devastation. It was a structure of carved wood and marble in the form of a pagoda, fifteen feet high and twenty-five wide, crawling with ornamental dragons. Four red columns supported a three-level roof of green shingles. The entryway's neon lights were lit, illuminating the inscriptions carved in the wood and marble: one proclaimed equality among human beings under the sky and the other wished a long life and happiness to the pedestrians. Weiss halted in front of the entrance and, repeating a ritual he enacted every time he prepared to cross under the arch, he read the inscription carved in the center of its highest point: "The dreams of every person who passes through this arch will be realized."

He outlined an ironic smile, crossed through the entryway, and entered Capón Street, crowded with shops and restaurants, whose entrances and façades displayed boughs of aromatic herbs as protection from calamities. A good number of men equipped with small lanterns placed on the end of a pole formed a curved line, simulating the body of a dragon: at the front went one man who carried the colorful head of the animal, and the man at the rear carried the tail. The men were dressed in red and white and spun in line, shaking the hanging lanterns to and fro, imitating the sinuous swagger of the winged serpent.

To avoid being run over by the human dragon, Weiss stepped up onto the sidewalk and headed to The House of Dreams, property of Mr. Siu Komt, an astrologer and amateur philosopher. Located a block above the arch, The House of Dreams was an old mansion with high ceilings and elaborate wood balconies that were cantilevered from its façade.

Weiss sounded the knocker on the heavy door, which opened a few seconds later. A boy let him in and led him along a corridor to the reception hall. From an adjacent room appeared Mr. Komt, a tall, thin, partly bald, wrinkled man who was stooped over from age. He greeted Weiss with a bow. Weiss removed his pistol from its shoulder holster and handed it over to him. Komt stored it in a closet, which he locked, and left the reception area followed by Weiss.

They entered a large room where there were several cots, occupied—all but one—by men in a dream state. All of them were serenely reclined, wrapped in comfortable blankets, with their mouths open, their eyes glazed, their gaze unfocused, smoking long pipes and enveloped amidst rings of intoxicating smoke. Komt led Weiss to the empty cot. He took off his coat, shirt, and shoes and lay down. Komt handed him the pipe. Weiss inhaled deeply as the old man stood up and, fixing his eyes on the captain, murmured in Chinese:

"Man only sees what he thinks is the truth; he doesn't see truth itself. And the truth is that everything we live is a dream."

Then the old man left the room. Weiss was already on the way to the world of dreams. He felt a tingling in his whole body, and he floated down to a zone where reality mixed with fantasy. He thought he saw himself on a ship, rocked by waves. The movements were so violent that he and the rest of the crew—children, adolescents, and old people—had to throw themselves to the deck so as not to fall overboard. Frightful convulsions tossed the ship, and the people—Chinese and Jews—were petrified as they prayed, resigned to die. Suddenly he saw himself outside the boat, standing in the street of a great city. The ground kept quaking and the windows of the houses were exploding, the glass embedding in the faces of the pedestrians. He knew he was in the midst of an earthquake that was not an earthquake. It had begun with the noise of a truck engine that arose from the mountains, occasionally interrupted by the strident chattering of the birds and the disquieting buzzing of insects, and now made a deafening roar like that of the tanks that as a child he had seen parading through the avenues of Berlin.

———————

Weiss got out of his car and headed to the house on the corner. He opened the door with his key. He greeted the guard who watched the entrance and went down a hallway. The lounge was lit with a dim, soothing light. Four well-dressed prostitutes, carefully made-up as if ready to go to a formal dance, were seated in navy-blue velvet armchairs. A couple danced to the beat of a bolero coming out of a record player. Another couple, seated at the bar, sipped their drinks. One of the women greeted the captain with a smile and another with a nod of her head as Weiss approached the bar.

The bartender Leopoldo placed a couple of wine glasses on the bar. He was a muscular, strapping indigenous man of about forty-five who towered over everyone in the room. Hair meticulously parted, with an exquisite tidiness about him, Leopoldo had a delicate touch that belied his obvious brute strength.

"Hey bro," greeted Weiss.

"Hey Simón," Leopoldo smiled warmly.

"Still scared?" teased the captain. "The earthquake shook you up, so I heard."

"Me? Right! It takes more than that to rattle me."

"Mmmmm... what's the fragrance you have on today? You smell just like the boss," teased Weiss.

"If you're lucky, maybe she'll give you some," answered Leopoldo.

Weiss set off down the hallway that led to Margarita's

bedroom. She was the brothel's owner and Leopoldo's sister. He opened the door. Weiss found her wearing a silk gown slip and sitting at her vanity table, dreamily putting on her make-up. She was a bronze-skinned Indian woman, about fifty, and exceptionally sensual. The two kissed, long and passionately.

"Slow in here tonight," he said.

"The earthquake has chased the customers away," she said, clutching herself to his chest. "Who can blame them?"

Weiss shrugged off his coat, and Margarita hung it in the closet with the other garments he habitually left in her bedroom. He placed his gun and holster on a rack jammed with high heels, and collapsed in an armchair. Margarita stood behind him, kneading his shoulders as he turned on the TV and, simultaneously it seemed, poured a white powder onto the glass top of the coffee table, cutting it into several lines. The front of the pool hall appeared on the TV screen, as did Sofía Galindo, along with her inquisitive voice:

"...the body of a Japanese man in the famous Shima Pool Hall. The man's throat was slashed and the body nailed to a table like a Christ."

Sofía continued talking while the camera panned and then zoomed in on the darkened entrance of the pool hall.

"The name of the deceased is Tokayoshi Takashima, co-owner of the establishment. All signs point to a rit-ual murder, even though, according to the famed captain Simón Weiss, who is heading the investigation with Lieutenant Kato Kanashiro..."

And in the apartment over the barbershop, Lieutenant Kanashiro and his father watched the news, closely following the young woman's words as if looking for some sign.

"The exact motive for the crime is still unknown, and it would be premature to conclude anything in that regard. Nonetheless, there is speculation that Takashima was murdered to steal the sixty thousand dollars he had received from his countrymen who all participated in a *tanomoshe*, or betting pool. This is common practice in the Japanese community of Lima, and many participate, forming private groups that pool a fixed quantity of money, with a share distributed by lottery every month."

And in his office, Inspector Castro Castro also watched the news, pacing from corner to corner.

"...Some suspect that the murderer or murderers may be among the other eleven participants in last May's pool. However, there is no solid basis to support this hypothesis, for few Japanese immigrants have perpetrated acts of that sort in Peru. Most of them, as many shopkeepers in the neighborhood will tell you, are simply hard-working and upstanding individuals..."

The confident Galindo smile flashed as she bowed her head just slightly. "Sofía Galindo reporting for Channel Five."

Weiss turned off the TV, muttering under his breath:

"Ah, Kato. So you forgot to tell me about the pool... What else are you hiding from me?"

Then he and Margarita bent over the table and, using two small paper tubes, snorted the white powder. She flipped a switch and a fluorescent light, something between rose pink and crimson, flooded the room. Taking the woman in his arms, he carried her to the bed where she undressed him, her hand stroking the right arm with its tattooed number.

"So you have a partner?" she asked.

"Castro Castro's orders," he answered, caressing her.

"You taking orders?"

"It was more of a request," he explained. "Besides, as you very well know, if you want to have your way, sometimes it's convenient to play along."

Weiss caressed her whole body, squeezing her ample breasts, her full thighs. Again and again their mouths melded into one lone breath, each more ardent and urgent than the last. Then he mounted her from behind and pulled violently on her hair.

"I like you a lot," he whispered.

Margarita emitted rhythmic moans, emerging from the depths of her being.

"Are you still my whore?" he asked, closing his eyes.

She moaned, rocking against him, focused on her pleasure.

"Say it."

"I'm still your whore."

"And you like it?"

"Yes."

"You like it or you love it?"

"I love it," she said, yielding to pleasure.

"My little whore," he said, closing his eyes. "How much do you like me?"

Suddenly, his hands slid around her waist, and clasped between her thighs like a claw. Panting, she grasped his arms and dug in with her nails. His face against hers, her cheeks were on fire.

"I don't like you at all," she whispered hoarsely, eyes flashing. "Not at all."

He was being absorbed by her, and he let himself be drawn inside further. He squeezed her tight, gripped by an ambivalent desire that at times seemed to turn into rage. "Then what?"

"I only love you," she half-cried.

Clutching each other and spinning as if into a bottomless pit, they climaxed. Both spent, they remained silent for a few minutes. Abruptly, he stood up, walked to the window, and began to open it.

"Don't," she stopped him. "Ever since the earthquake there is a strange smell everywhere."

"All of Lima smells like a woman in heat," he muttered.

"Like a woman in heat?" she said, irritated, sweat glistening on her brow.

"I mean like *my* woman in heat," he replied quickly.

Weiss went up to her and kissed her passionately. Then he picked up the guitar that was propped against the wall, lay back against the headboard of the bed, and began to strum it, softly. Margarita rested her head on his thigh and closed her eyes. After several chords, she turned over and looked at him.

"How sad. I never heard you play this one before," she said.

"'Forest Flowers'" he said. And then he added: "'Love's loss drove me crazy.'"

Margarita looked at him curiously. Weiss stopped playing.

"That's how the song ends," he explained.

Margarita's eyes shone with a flicker of worry.

"I had a horrible dream last night," she said.

"Tell me," he said.

"You were with another woman... kissing her," she said, with a shiver.

"And I'm sure you tore her eyes out," he mocked.

Weiss started the song again but Margarita's desperate voice interrupted him.

"Simón, do you still love me?"

Weiss looked at her.

"Twenty years together and you're still asking me?"

"You love me or you're just horny for me?" she insisted.

"I love you and I'm horny for you," he said, tenderly.

Weiss began strumming the guitar again.

"Twenty years... Do you remember our first time?" she said.

"You liked me so much that you didn't charge me," he answered with affection.

"You told me that it was your birthday... that you turned twenty and that it was your first time. You lied to me."

"It was my first time."

"But you weren't twenty."

Weiss stopped playing.

"Would you have fallen in love with me if I told you I was fifteen?" he asked, smiling.

Margarita asked again:

"And you, did you fall in love with me?"

Weiss strummed a few chords.

"As soon as I set eyes on you," he said.

"That's what you say," she protested. For some reason, whenever he stood in her room, undressed, she invariably searched for the number on his arm, hoping it might have disappeared, been erased by their love. "But you had a special need. I sensed it from the start, but I didn't care."

Weiss stopped playing; his eyebrows furrowed:

"What are you talking about?"

"Do I have to spell it out for you? It's been twenty years and you still wake up in the middle of the night crying for your mommy, and calling her a whore."

"They're just dreams. They have nothing to do with us."

"Simón, I don't care why you feel what you feel for me...

29

but I won't fool myself. You know what you look for in me, so don't play dumb."

"Seems to work for you well enough..."

"I just want to make you happy."

Margarita opened her arms, inviting him back to her. Weiss put the guitar aside and, with his eyes closed, as if buried in a dream, surrendered meekly to her embrace. She clung to him, afraid of something she knew intimately, even if she couldn't quite recognize what it was.

WEDNESDAY, THE 3RD

WEISS AWOKE, STRAIGHTENING up like an uncoiling spring and stifling a moan. Margarita woke up, held him, and little by little calmed him down. In the dream, the scorpion's face had turned into his adoptive father's face.

"Before he plunges the stinger into his own back," he says to me, "'Remember the ekdesh.'"

"Ekdesh?" Margarita asked.

"It has to be Yiddish," said Weiss.

The telephone's ring interrupted him, like the croak of a bad omen. He picked up the receiver, still shaken by the dream.

"Weiss," Inspector Castro Castro said urgently. "I just spoke with your mother. They've just found one of her boarders dead."

"Where?"

"In his room at the boarding house."

Weiss already had a cigarette lit in his mouth, "Circumstances?"

"Not totally clear. Everything right now points to suicide."

"I'm on my way."

"Weiss."

"Yes"

"This is a courtesy call. I've put Kanashiro officially in charge of the case."

"That seems like a perfect solution, Inspector."

"Anything new with the pool hall case? Is it true what the Galindo girl said? Where the hell did she get the information about the lottery?"

"I don't know, Inspector."

"Well, that's precisely why I had Kanashiro work with you."

"My feelings exactly, Inspector."

The inspector hung up and Weiss dialed a number.

"Kanashiro, meet me in an hour at the Atlantic."

––––––––––

Lieutenant Kanashiro was searching like a madman through his father's closet. He knew his father did not own a safe, but he remembered that a few days before he had seen him placing one in the closet of his room, seemingly hiding it. At the time, distracted by thoughts of Sofía, he had thought little of it. But now? Giving up, the lieutenant went downstairs, where Mr. Kanashiro was reading a Japanese-language newspaper. Across the room, his assistant was cutting a customer's hair. The lieutenant signaled his father to follow him upstairs.

In his father's bedroom, the lieutenant showed him the closet and asked him about the safe. Mr. Kanashiro's mouth tensed in surprise. He turned and made an attempt to return downstairs, shaking the paper he still held. The lieutenant insisted he stay, and eventually the elder Kanashiro relented, lifting up some planks from the floor, and producing a small metal box.

"Takashima gave it to me for safekeeping, but he didn't give me the combination," he admitted.

"The man was nailed alive to a table, father. Then they slit his throat and bled him out like cattle."

Mr. Kanashiro shook his head sadly.

"And you didn't think you should tell me about this?"

The lieutenant took a piece of paper out of his jacket pocket, where he had jotted down the combination found in the pool hall, and opened the safe, against his father's admonitions.

"He warned me not to say anything," Mr. Kanashiro muttered. "My life and yours depended on it—that's what he said."

The safe did not contain money, but it was full of photos, newspaper clippings, and documents that revealed what the lieutenant wanted to know. The first thing he took out was a photo of Takashima in a military uniform, accompanied by other Japanese officers in a prison camp. A newspaper clipping showed Takashima in court in front of a group of officers. "Damning testimony," read the caption.

It continued: "Tokayoshi Takashima, a captain in the Japanese army, served in a prison camp in the Philippines and, once the war was over, testified against his superior, the camp's chief colonel, convicted in absentia as a war criminal."

The lieutenant took out a thin piece of paper, folded carefully. He opened it, and discovered that it was written in Japanese characters.

"It is a note signed by Takashima," Mr. Kanashiro said.

"What does it say?" asked the lieutenant.

Mr. Kanashiro began to translate:

"Colonel Kengo Tanaka, commander of a prison camp in the Philippines and convicted in absentia as a war criminal, is living in Lima with a new identity and a different face. I've seen him in my pool hall and recognized him thanks to the mark he bears on his left calf, which resembles a scorpion."

The lieutenant gave a stifled whistle and remained motionless for an instant. Then he scratched his head, perhaps wondering if he was dreaming, or as if he were stunned by the weight of these coincidences.

"You're kidding," said Weiss.

They were seated at a table at the Café Atlantic, in the middle of Lima's Main Square. Weiss smoked and drank a coffee. Kanashiro sipped a Coke. It was a rare sunny day.

"I immediately remembered your dream, Captain. I thought I was hallucinating." And pointing with his index finger at a word in the note left by Takashima, he added: "But here it is, very clear: sasori."

"Which means scorpion in Japanese," said Weiss.

"Isn't it incredible?"

"So they didn't kill him for the money," added Weiss, to himself.

"You were right, Captain," the lieutenant let out a sigh of relief. "The safe contained something more important than money."

Pigeons exploded up into the sky and, for a moment, blocked out the sun.

"One other thing, Lieutenant."

Kanashiro paused with the Coke at his lips.

"This is the last time you hide something from me," said Weiss in his most serious and cutting tone.

"Captain, what happened is that—"

"The last time. Clear?"

"Clear, Captain, and I'm grateful," exclaimed Kanashiro, flushing despite the cool soda he clutched near his temple.

Weiss stood up, tossed a few bills on the table, and left the café, trailed by Kanashiro. Soon after, the sun left as well.

———————

Huamani and Bocanegra waited for them at the main door to Esther the Pole's boarding house. Weiss, a man of many keys, opened the big door and let his team into an enormous courtyard, paved with stones, with elegant columns of fine carved wood, and Italian mosaics. A marble staircase led up to the second floor, long since shuttered and unoccupied due to the cost of heating and upkeep. Nevertheless, Esther's boarding house, known also as The House of Thirteen Doors, was an imposing structure from colonial times, situated on Soledad Street, and two blocks from the Government Palace. Its main door faced the Church of San Francisco, and three blocks up was Bolívar Square, which housed Congress and the Museum of the Inquisition.

Having barely arrived in Peru, Weiss's adoptive father had gone to that boarding house looking for work. And not only did he find work, but a new love. Shortly thereafter, he and Esther the Pole got married and little Simón found both a new mother and a new home.

Weiss and his group crossed the courtyard and entered the house through a grand door, out of which emerged loud but unintelligible voices.

Esther appeared clad in a gown of fine silk and high heels. She was a mid-sixties woman, red-headed and attractive. In her right hand she waved a wrinkled and yellowed document, and she was shouting riotously at a man— a bureaucrat from the Judiciary—who was backing up towards the exit until he bumped into Weiss and his crew.

"Here is the Minister of Justice's signature, in his own handwriting! He gave it to me! In return for my services. And do you know what I turned it into? The best boarding house in Lima! A destination for visitors from around the world! And now you come to take it away from me? No, sir, nobody takes away the Pole's house. Get out!"

"Lady, please, I'm only following orders," the functionary defended himself, more and more out of breath. "This house has been declared a national landmark and it belongs to the people. You have a month to return it to the state."

"Get out, I said!"

The government official left the house looking scared, and Esther slammed the door after him. Weiss hugged his stepmother affectionately and tried to make eye contact with her.

"Mom, calm down..."

"Those bastards! Trying to take my house away from me, my house!" she said, and then turning to pet Weiss's cheek with the back of her hand. Weiss pulled her hand away, and Esther concluded, with a slight tremor in her voice: "You've come about poor Mr. Kleimer? What a terrible thing, my God, nothing like this has ever happened here."

"And Dad?" inquired Weiss.

"In the library, with his head buried in his books. Gustaff, your son is here!"

Gustaff Haas emerged with a book in his hand and eyes distant and mild, as if the shouting and yelling had not reached his ears. He and Weiss embraced affectionately.

"I see you're still having problems with the house," said Weiss.

"They won't stop. Most likely we'll have to move the boarding house some place else," said Haas.

"I've told you that they'll evict me over my dead body," Esther protested.

"And that classmate of yours from the Leoncio Prado who works closely with the General? Simón, speak to him," Haas urged his son, tucking the book under his arm. "Tell him I'm a leftist, like the General..."

"I'll see what I can do. But for now let's take care of business. Lieutenant Kanashiro here is in charge of the investigation."

"What? Why not you?" asked Haas, looking worried.

"The rules don't allow it," answered Weiss.

"And why didn't you insist? When Jews are involved, everything should stay in the family."

"Dad, we're not in Germany anymore."

To keep the others from understanding, Haas spoke in Yiddish.

"But Germany can be anywhere, my son."

"Don't speak to me in Yiddish. You know it's vanished from my memory. By the way, what does ekdesh mean?"

"Ekdesh?" Haas thought a moment. "Scorpion."

Weiss smiled wryly. "Of course it does."

"Why son?"

"No reason," and Weiss motioned to Kanashiro to take over the investigation.

"Sir, please show us where the body was found," said the lieutenant.

Haas led them down a hallway to the victim's bedroom, worry clouding his face.

"Who found the body?" asked the lieutenant.

"Me. I found it," called Esther. "This morning I took Mr. Kleimer his breakfast. I knocked on the door several times, and since he wasn't opening I went to get my husband."

"We got tired of knocking. I had to force the door open because it was locked from the inside. I went in and there was Maurice hanging from one of the ceiling rafters," said Haas.

"It was horrible," added Esther.

"What can you tell us about Mr. Kleimer?" asked the lieutenant.

"He was our new boarder," Esther said. "He'd been with us only a few weeks."

"Four, to be exact," said Haas. "He came from Argentina

with his granddaughter, a girl married to a Peruvian, also Jewish. That's all we know."

"Well, thanks," the lieutenant said.

Kanashiro went over to Huamani and Bocanegra.

"Wait here."

Esther walked down the hallway that led to the kitchen and Haas stood beside the door. Kanashiro invited the Captain to enter.

The room was in perfect order, except for a chair that had tipped onto the floor. The dead man, dressed in pants and a long-sleeve shirt, hung from one of the rafters. Weiss stared a long time at him and felt a fleeting vision come to mind, much like the one he had had a couple of nights before, when he saw a man swinging by his neck— like a replica of the one before his eyes—hanging from a rafter, the body itself stiff, but swaying like a pendulum. He had been a detective since he was 22 years old—now he was 35— and this was the first time that he had had a premonition.

Weiss snapped back to reality and immediately began to inspect the room. He half-closed the door, studied it, looked for anything on the floor, beneath the bed, and then among the few pieces of furniture. Kanashiro repeated the captain's actions, in nearly the exact same order, beginning with the inside of the door.

"This was not a suicide," pronounced Weiss.

"The murderer—or murderers—locked the room from

the outside," said Kanashiro. "But how did they get into the building?"

"Maybe through that hole in the ceiling," said Weiss, raising his eyes. "Still, whoever wanted this to look like a suicide wasn't much of a pro."

Weiss lowered his gaze and then immediately, as if someone had slapped him on the back of the neck, returned his eyes to the ceiling.

"What's that up there?" he said, pointing toward one of the beams.

Kanashiro quickly climbed on top of a dresser. Weiss passed him the dead man's cane propped in a corner, which the lieutenant used to free a piece of paper trapped between the rafter and the ceiling. The paper floated down in slow motion. Weiss snared it from the air. Unfolded it. Read in silence. Then he left the room, followed by the lieutenant.

"Dad, listen to this," called the captain, his voice so animated that Kanashiro could almost picture his boss as a youngster. Almost. Weiss read: "To the attention of the President of the Jewish Association of Argentina. The Butcher of Sachsenhausen, Captain of the Gestapo, Gerd Kroneg is living in Lima. Three days ago I saw him at the ballet a few minutes before the performance ended. I went looking for him, but Kroneg had already disappeared. I have reported the incident to the police; I spoke to a captain whose name I don't recall. He told me they would investigate the case and would get back to me, but so far they have not done so..."

Weiss checked the back of the paper. "That's all it says."

He stood still, holding the note, stupefied as did Haas. Something had joined them in the air.

"Gerd Kroneg in Lima! Fate has placed him in our path, Dad. And Maurice Kleimer... do you remember him?"

"No, not at all," replied Haas breathlessly.

Weiss waved the note at Kanashiro.

"Here's the motive, Lieutenant."

Kanashiro approached Huamani and Bocanegra.

"You can go in now."

Huamani and Bocanegra stepped into the crime scene, and Kanashiro returned to the courtyard, where he began interviewing the other boarders and the cleaning ladies. Weiss took the opportunity to walk down the hall and slip into a washroom, where he unpacked a small mirror, onto which he tapped a few lines of white powder. Two bumps, and the new energy, concentrated behind his eyes but spreading throughout his body, rushed up to meet him like an overenthusiastic friend.

He leaned his forehead on the glass. In his mind he saw the swinging body of the hanged man, and a voice, emerging from the morning's dream, but also from some hidden place in his memory, hammered his brain, in time with his racing pulse: "Ekdesh, ekdesh, ekdesh." He needed air. As he exited, his gaze met Esther's, who stood in the hallway, waiting.

"When are you going to quit that garbage? It's going to kill you," she reproached. Her words were harsh but the tone was gentle and she sighed with resignation, caressing his wet brow.

"Stop worrying. Nothing's going to happen to me," said Weiss, pinching her cheek.

Then back down the hallway went Weiss, his step-mother watching him as he walked away, shaking her head. When he reached the reception hall, Kanashiro had already dismissed the boarders and cleaning ladies.

"Blind and deaf, Captain: No one saw or heard anything.

The coroner entered, followed by two men pushing a gurney.

"Where's the corpse?" asked the coroner, agitated. "Counting this one, I've had to remove four bodies today. And it's not like they pay me per body! Let's see, who is going to sign?"

Kanashiro went over to sign the order. Weiss went to say good-bye to Haas. Then Kanashiro did the same. Weiss hugged his father and left, followed by the lieutenant. Passing the kitchen, Weiss poked his head in. Esther the Pole was giving final instructions to the cook for lunch.

"Mom, I'm leaving."

The Pole walked to him.

"Stay for lunch," she said.

"Today won't work for me. Some other time. I promise."

"You're always running. Take care of yourself, son. Sleep is the best thing. Make sure she lets you."

Weiss smiled and gave her a peck on the cheek. Kanashiro said goodbye, and both men went out to the courtyard, Weiss with a new cigarette dangling from his lip.

"The day before yesterday a Japanese man was murdered, and last night they killed a Jew. What does that say to you?" asked Weiss.

"I don't know, Captain. What?"

"They're hunting us down, Kato."

"That sounds..."

"Paranoid? Asking a Jew not to get paranoid is like asking..."

"...a scorpion not to sting," finished Kanashiro.

"Exactly. It's in their nature. It's what they say about Scorpios."

"Not all of them, Captain, there are exceptions. It depends on the rising sign."

"Ahh," Weiss blew a ring of smoke over his partner's face. "So you believe in the power of the stars?"

Without giving him a chance to answer, Weiss swung open the heavy gate and went out.

––––––––––

The forensics doctor opened the door and, followed by

Weiss and Kanashiro, entered a long, wide corridor where a good number of tables were wheeled against both walls with their corpses, some covered with sheets and others half-exposed, awaiting burial. They were a few of the earthquake's victims.

The corpses, and their smell, inspired a fleeting vision in Weiss. He saw rows of decomposing bodies piled up along a trench in a concentration camp.

The doctor pointed to the rows of bodies and said:

"The problem is that the relatives don't have the money to buy coffins, and since we're out of formaldehyde some bodies are starting to decompose. The authorities have set tomorrow morning as the deadline to bury the corpses. That's why many are burying their loved ones in common graves on the outskirts of the city. It's really terrible, but what can be done?"

They arrived at a door labeled FORENSIC LAB; the doctor opened it and they entered. The doctor went directly over to two side-by-side tables and uncovered the first, where Tokayoshi Takashima's body lay.

"This one bled first from his wrists and his feet, they definitely slit his throat afterwards," he informed. Next, he approached the other table and uncovered Kleimer's corpse.

"This one has been dead about twenty-four hours and there's something odd about him."

The doctor took hold of the dead man's right arm and

twisted it, revealing the tattoo of a number—55538—and, next to it, the figure of a small scorpion.

Weiss clutched his forearm and, his face altered, sank into another vision. He saw a man violently dragging another man by his hair and, with his other hand, beating his back with a cudgel. The arm of the man who held the cudgel bore the same number and the same scorpion figure as those tattooed on the dead man's forearm.

Weiss came back to reality, his forehead beaded with sweat. Kanashiro silently observed him. The doctor spoke again:

"Cause of death? Asphyxiation. But not by strangulation. We found a good dose of barbiturates in his blood."

"And someone who is going to hang himself doesn't take sleeping pills," said Weiss.

"They wanted us to think that this scorpion committed suicide, Captain," Kanashiro said.

"Well, the scorpion is the only animal that kills itself... Except, of course, for man," noted the doctor, raising his eyebrows.

Weiss stepped away from the table and went back out to the hall. Kanashiro followed him.

"This is unbelievable, Captain. Another scorpion."

"Kato, for now, not a word to the inspector about this, eh!"

"Don't worry, Captain. I'm under your command."

Weiss looked across the corridor and spotted a man and woman. The young woman, about twenty-five years old, ethereally attractive, looked like an apparition. She was profoundly downcast, and the man, about fifty, with a mustache and a wispy beard, impeccably dressed, held her up by the arm.

Upon noticing the rows of corpses along both sides of the corridor, the girl stopped still, impacted by the spectacle. Weiss went over to her. As the girl became more and more visible, Weiss's expression grew stranger and stranger. When he finally saw her up close he was invaded by another vision. In front of a barracks, a couple of German soldiers were pushing several women inside. The women were made up and dressed in street clothes, not in the striped pajamas worn by camp prisoners. The man with the tattoo was prodding them with a cudgel, while with his other arm he held up, as if protecting her, a girl whose face incredibly resembled that of the young woman before his eyes.

Weiss felt himself strangely drawn to the girl. He paid no attention to the man who accompanied her. His entire being was focused on her. He guessed she was Maurice Kleimer's granddaughter. He took a few steps forward and held her hand. She raised her head, looked at his eyes, and felt something she could not explain. He pulled her toward the forensic lab.

"Come this way," he said.

"Hey, where are you taking her?" said the man, alarmed.

The man tried to stop them but, at a signal from Weiss,

Kanashiro blocked his way.

"Mr. Pomerov? Don't worry, it's just so she can identify the body. Come with me, I want to ask you a few questions."

Pomerov tried to blow him off, but the lieutenant insisted. Confused, Pomerov saw Weiss and Olga enter the forensic lab and the door closing behind them.

"I demand you let me through. I'm her husband," he protested.

"Only one person is permitted to enter at a time," the lieutenant explained.

Kanashiro took him by the arm and Pomerov let himself be led, still protesting and looking back at the forensic lab.

Inside the forensic lab, with tears running down her cheeks, Olga hugged her grandfather's body. Weiss drew close to the girl and stood behind her, very close to her body, listening to the rhythm of her breathing.

"Is it true that he took his own life?" she asked.

"No," he answered.

"Are you sure?"

"Yes."

"Then who? Why?"

"I don't know yet."

Olga turned around and looked into his eyes, comforted by the captain's confident tone of voice.

"Promise me that the murderers won't get away with this," she said.

"I promise," he said.

Breathing anxiously, Olga rested her head on the captain's chest. He stroked her hair, slow, sweetly. Then he covered her breasts with his hands, and she let him caress her. At that moment, Kanashiro popped his head in. Seeing them, he quickly closed the door again.

Weiss and Olga went out to the corridor. As soon as he saw them, Pomerov ran toward her.

"Are you all right, dear? They didn't let me go in," he said, pulling his wife away from the captain. She seemed oblivious to what was happening. She headed toward the exit, not looking at her husband.

"If you'd like, you may go in," said Weiss.

"Who are you?" asked Pomerov.

"I am Captain Weiss."

"Weiss? Simón Weiss? The detective?"

Weiss blushed. It pleased him that people recognized his well-earned reputation, but he still couldn't help getting embarrassed.

"Is what the lieutenant said true? That it wasn't a suicide?" Pomerov asked.

"That's right."

"Are there any leads?"

"Do you know anything that might be useful to us?" Weiss asked.

"I already told the lieutenant everything I know."

"Good."

"Captain, more than twenty-four hours have passed and

the body..." said Pomerov.

"I've already given the order," Weiss interjected.

"Thank you. Keep me informed," said Pomerov. Then he headed toward the forensic lab.

"Twenty-four hours? What does that mean?" Kanashiro asked.

"We Jews must bury our dead within 24 hours," Weiss explained.

The captain signaled him that it was time for them to leave. They went out to the street. Across the way a black Cadillac was parked. Olga sat in the back seat while the chauffeur leaned against the vehicle.

"Wait for me in the car," Weiss ordered Kanashiro, moving toward the Cadillac. Olga lowered the window, handed him a piece of paper, and raised the glass.

Weiss read to himself:

"I live on the San Isidro Olive Grove, at 125 Guahananí Street. You can come whenever you like."

The captain stashed the note in his pocket and headed back to his car. Just then Pomerov emerged and motioned to his chauffeur, who opened the car door for him. Pomerov sat down next to his wife.

Weiss had already started driving off. As he passed by the Cadillac he kept his eyes fixed on the back seat. Kanashiro remained immutable, not looking at or saying anything.

———————

Under the watchful gaze of the conquistador Francisco Pizarro—on horseback, his sword unsheathed, and sporting his demoniacal warrior's helmet—Weiss showed his police badge, and the guard permitted him to enter the Government Palace, located to one side of the Plaza de Armas, scarcely a half block, on the diagonal, from the cathedral. At that hour the palace cut a gray silhouette across the setting sun.

A soldier, carrying a rifle, escorted Weiss across a broad and luxurious atrium, which was dimly lit. They came to a corridor lined with offices on both sides, protected by armed soldiers. They walked to the end of the hall, arriving at an office door that displayed a sign:

ISAAC MONTORO
CHIEF OF INTELLIGENCE SERVICE

The soldier stood to one side of the door, and Weiss knocked. Montoro's voice resounded from within:

"Come in!"

Weiss entered. At that moment, two generals and an admiral—from the Army, Air Force, and Navy— were leaving Montoro's office, each saluting him on their way out the door. Montoro then turned to meet Weiss with a broad smile and open arms. He was a man of about forty, tall, handsome, athletic, with a bearing that reflected his intelligence and, even more than that, his astuteness.

The two friends warmly threw their arms around each other. Montoro went back to his desk, and Weiss began to check behind the paintings and under the shelves.

"Do you mind telling me what you're looking for?" Montoro inquired.

"You wouldn't be taping me, would you?" answered Weiss, looking behind an armoire with mock suspicion.

"Brother, don't get paranoid. Come on, sit down," said Montoro.

"That's the second time today that someone has told me that."

"Told you what?"

"Not to get paranoid."

Weiss sat down, took out a little plastic bag from his coat, placed a bit of white powder on top of the glass table, and separated it into a pair of fine lines. He offered the plate to Montoro, who waved it off. Weiss shrugged and bent his head over and, using a small paper funnel, sniffed hard.

"You're hooked on the stuff," Montoro observed.

"I don't deny it. But it's the only way to face Peru… and the world. And besides, you need something else too," Weiss said, with an ironic smile. "For balance."

"What?"

"'Divine drug, eternal balm, opium and dreams,'" answered Weiss, singing a few lines of the famous waltz by Felipe Pinglo. And then he added:

"One of these days you must come with me, Isaac. Or are you afraid?"

"Of course not! It's just that that stuff goes against the ideals of our revolution."

Weiss scoffed at the notion of ideals and snorted again.

"Not to mention our program to transform Peru," Montoro added.

"Only with cocaine will we be able to transform Peru," replied Weiss.

"You're mad, Simón, as usual. Transformation can only be achieved through revolution, you know that as well as I."

"And dictatorships," said Weiss.

Montoro cast his gaze at the portrait of General Velasco that was hanging on the wall to one side of his desk. His eyes beamed with admiration.

"Everything the general does is to prevent a fratricidal war. That's why you have to come and work with me, Simón. You'll be my right-hand man."

"I'm perfectly fine where I am," Weiss declined.

"Simón, the revolution has many enemies, and I need a man like you."

"Again, I'm perfectly fine where I am," Weiss cut him off. "And I'm going to give you a piece of advice: be careful your office doesn't turn into a Gestapo. People are starting to talk about you as a sinister man."

"I only pretend to be one," Montoro smiled quickly.

"You should be careful with what you pretend to be," said Weiss, his own smile a melancholy one. "Sometimes you end up becoming just that."

Montoro lit Weiss's cigarette and then his own. He then turned to reviewing the folders sitting on his desk, showing Weiss the photo of Kengo Tanaka in a colonel's uniform.

"Kengo Tanaka is a war criminal. He entered Peru in 1945. He's had his face changed and his name now is Toshiro Sakura. He deals in the trafficking of girls of all races and backgrounds. He'll turn your daughter into a geisha without batting an eye. He's placed girls in brothels all over the country."

He paused to inhale his cigarette and continued:

"He hangs out at the Lotus Flower, a brothel. Be very careful when you speak to him. He is guarded by two or three karatekas. Your partner teach you that term yet? Whatever you call them, they're highly skilled killers, and they don't let him out of their sights."

"And Kroneg?"

"We have no one in our files under that name. But there are a couple of likely candidates who might be using an alias. Johann Müller, for example, entered Peru just after the end of the war, and keeps in touch with several ex-Nazis living in Peru. He's an arms dealer. He sells them to everyone and anyone, including the government."

Montoro paused again to review a folder, tip some ash into an ashtray, and then continued:

"He has a mansion in Barranco. He lives there with his butler, also German. Müller is not known to have bodyguards. He doesn't need them because he is protected by operatives within the National Police."

"The police?"

"That's right. At your own HQ there's a captain... Aránguiz. Do you know him?"

"An asshole."

"And extremely dangerous," warned Montoro. "A criminal disguised as a policeman. And a traitor to Peru. He's sold secrets to Ecuador and Chile regarding the selling of weapons, secrets that Müller passes to him and that he's also sold to the CIA. He would sell his own mother. Be careful, Simón."

"And why is he still on the loose?"

"There are things we need him for. But we'll get him."

"So Müller's off limits then?" asked Weiss.

Montoro stood up and walked over to the captain, putting a hand on his shoulder.

"He needs to stay where he is for now. It's important. Do you understand, Simón?"

Weiss slipped free of the hand, "Any protections on Tanaka I should know about, apart from his bodyguards? Anything your sacred government wants him for?"

Montoro looked hurt. "You look bad, my friend. What's happening?"

"Things feel like they are catching up to me. I'm remembering things. Things I didn't know I had stored in my head."

Weiss looked at Montoro and shrugged his shoulders, not knowing what else to say. He walked a few steps toward the door, stopped, and turned halfway around, the white powder coursing through him suddenly.

"I have a message from my old man: he wants me to tell you that he's a leftist, like the general, and that they should stop fucking with him over his house."

"His house?"

"Because it's been declared a historical landmark, the State wants to take it away from him."

"A good man, your dad. Tell him not to worry. I'll make sure they leave him alone."

"Thanks," said Weiss.

Montoro grabbed Weiss by the shoulders again,

"Simón, remember what I've said. And watch out for Aránguiz."

Montoro embraced Weiss, who stiffly acquiesced. Then Montoro opened the door, and Weiss went out into the corridor.

"See the captain to the exit," Montoro ordered the soldier posted to one side of the door, and then Weiss left the National Palace.

That night, Weiss dreamed of a somber, slate sky overhead and the front of a barracks where a couple of German soldiers were pushing several women inside. The women were made up and dressed in street clothes, not in the striped pajamas worn by camp prisoners. The man with the tattoo was prodding them with a cudgel, while with his other arm he held up, as if protecting her, a girl whose face incredibly resembled that of the young woman he had met at the morgue.

He awoke knowing what had to happen, and picked up the telephone to call Kanashiro.

THURSDAY, THE 4TH

SHADOWS FELL OVER the cliff that faced the sea as fog rolled in from the Pacific, and met the city. Inside the Channel 5 news van, Sofía Galindo and Lieutenant Kanashiro were pressed tightly against each other, achieving a prolonged orgasm together. Through the windshield they watched the fog coming in.

"I can't wait for us to be married and to make love in a bed, our bed, like normal people," Sofía said, pulling her skirt back over lean brown thighs.

"Your parents don't want you to marry a Japanese man."

"To hell with my parents," the girl protested.

"That's easy to say in this van," Kanashiro laughed.

"New winds are blowing, Kato. Don't you watch the news?" She pinched his bicep fiercely. "Besides, my parents know that you're only half Japanese. Your mother was just like me, right?"

"Yes," he answered.

"Yes what? Say it," she pressed her naked torso against his.

"A pretty little Indian girl," he added with a smile.

"And she had you, a handsome little Japanese Indian baby," she teased, flashing her famous smile.

"That's not the way your folks see me. To them I'm a Jap," he said with regret.

"Don't be so hard on them. Soon they'll realize that the best thing for me is you."

Kanashiro shook his head helplessly. Sofía watched a plane as it approached with its lights blinking through the fog.

"We're going to have to elope, aren't we?" she sighed, only half-kidding. "Look, here comes a plane. Where do you think it's going? When it passes over us, let's jump and catch it. Come on."

Sofía put on her blouse, took Kanashiro's hand and they got out of the van. As the plane passed over their heads, Sofía leaped, as if to snare it with her hand.

"Kato, jump!"

But she only managed to grab a fistful of air.

"You know very well that I can't abandon my old man," he said with conviction.

"If they promoted you to captain, my parents..."

Kanashiro shook his head, "These two cases won't let me think about anything else beyond tomorrow."

The young people drew near the cliff edge. From there

they could see La Punta, lit up like a rosary.

"Any new leads?" she asked.

"That's just what I wanted to talk to you about," he answered.

At that instant another plane passed over them, and as the lieutenant began to speak Sofía leaned close to hear him over the jet noise.

Clad in an elegant dress, Margarita readied herself in front of her vanity table before going out to the bar. She watched Weiss's reflection in her mirror, as he slumped in her armchair separating his white powder into lines, and glancing up at the television, at the news story Sofía Galindo was reporting.

"...the National Police continue investigating the brutal murder of Tokayoshi Takashima, which happened on the day of the earthquake. Police have discarded the theory that Takashima was killed to steal the lottery money, since he was not the winner of the lucrative purse, as was originally thought. At this point, thanks to a note left by the victim in a safe that is in police custody, suspicion has fallen on a certain Kengo Tanaka..."

And in his office at the Lotus Flower, Kengo Tanaka was also attentively following the news. Flanked by two geisha girls—one white and one black—who dispensed languid, feigned caresses, Tanaka watched the screen with a dour expression on his face. Standing behind him, Tojishiko Sato, Fujimoto, and Nagakata, his bodyguards, kept their eyes fixed on the TV set, too.

"...ex-colonel of the Japanese army convicted in absentia of being a war criminal. According to the note left by Takashima, a former captain of the Japanese army and witness for the prosecution against the colonel, Kengo Tanaka lives in Lima under a new name and face. Nonetheless, according to information provided by Captain Simón Weiss, proof of his true identity lies in that safe, which is in the hands of the police."

Tanaka signaled to his bodyguard. Nagakata went to him and put his ear to the colonel's lips. At once Nagakata and Fujimoto left the office.

Weiss stood up and began to pace like a caged animal from one side of the room to the other as Sofía kept reporting the story they had given her:

"In other news, yesterday the body of an elderly Jewish man was found hanging from a rafter in his room in a boarding house known as The House of Thirteen Doors."

Weiss lit a cigarette off the dying butt of his last one.

And at The House of Thirteen Doors, Gustaff Haas and Esther listened anxiously to the young reporter's words.

"...it is known that the deceased was named Maurice Kleimer and that he had been in Lima only a few weeks, coming from Argentina. At first it was thought to be a suicide, but thanks to a note left by the victim, suspicion now rests on a certain Gerd Kroneg, an ex-captain of the Gestapo."

And flanked by Aránguiz and his butler, Johann Müller watched the news in disbelief. At his feet lay an enormous Doberman, with fidgety eyes.

"Lieutenant Kato Kanashiro, who is in charge of the investigation, has reported that said note locates the ex-captain in Lima, but his new identity is not known. It is only known that Israeli agents may be looking for Kroneg because of crimes committed at the Sachsenhausen concentration camp during the Second World War. Sofía Galindo reporting, Channel Five."

Weiss turned the TV off. Then he snorted the white powder he had prepared. After a while he went over to Margarita, kissed her passionately, and opened the door to leave, but Margarita's compelling voice stopped him.

"Simón, what's wrong?"

"Nothing," he answered, lowering his eyes.

"Are you sure?"

"Yes, sure..."

But Olga Pomerov's face haunted him, and the captain kissed his mistress tenderly but with closed eyes and left. Margarita went back to the mirror. A curse, she feared, was coming.

Weiss entered the lounge bar. There were several customers, some hidden away in easy chairs, others perched at the bar, but each accompanied by one of the women who worked at the place. And each watched the television, as it showed its macabre and heartrending scenes of the earthquake. The announcer's voice sounded pitiful:

"This is a panorama of Yungay after Sunday's devastating earthquake. In other areas punished by the quake, angry mobs have begun to loot shops and drug stores, due to the lack of food, water, and medicine."

Weiss gestured to Leopoldo.

"Brother, pour me a pisco."

Leopoldo served him, and Weiss drained the glass.

He pointed to the glass for a refill and Leopoldo obeyed; when he finished pouring the liquor Weiss grabbed his hand. "Let's keep it close, shall we?"

"Drowning your sorrows?" Leopoldo chided the detective. "It can't be for love. I know how much Margarita loves you. You don't even see love like that in novels."

"And I don't deserve it," said Weiss in an opaque voice.

"What do you mean? What have you done?" Leopoldo's huge chest expanded and leaned across the bar.

Weiss remained silent, with his eyes buried in the bottom of his glass.

"Be very careful with what you do, Simón. My sister—you treat her like a queen, or you deal with me!" Leopoldo warned in a heated whisper near his ear.

Weiss filled his glass again and drank the contents in one gulp. Then he stood up and switched off the TV. With the customers and the girls watching, he made his way over to a darkened corner of the lounge, which had been converted into a stage near the far end of the bar. From the shadows, Weiss strummed the guitar:

"Reclining on regal cushions,
A beautiful princess smiles provocatively at me,
Like a queen mentioned in fairy tales,
Bedazzling she appears before me."

When she heard the first stanza, Margarita came out into the hallway.

"Her eyes are fiery, they drive me mad;
She loves me and offers frenzy,
In her face of cherub or Nereid
Are divined desires of endless bliss."

Weiss's voice seemed to crack, but he continued:

"Divine drug, eternal balm,
Opium and dreams give us life;
I breathe the smoke that bestows grandeur
And when I dream, I am born anew."

An uncontrollable desolation seized Margarita's soul.

"I become owner of countless riches,
Lovely women fill my harem
And surrounded by them, I, almost asleep,
Sipping joys, drinking flattery,
I lie in the arms of a woman."

Suddenly, Weiss stopped singing and while still bathed in the audience's applause, he rested the guitar against the wall and left the place.

FRIDAY, THE 5TH

THE HOME OF Olga and Harry Pomerov was nicely situated in the San Isidro Olive Grove. For the past few days, the homes in these woods had been invaded by rats and cockroaches that, terrorized by the earthquake, in turn terrorized the neighbors at night, especially the children. The Pomerov residence was a two-story, modern and luxurious house.

Weiss parked his car alongside the garden and walked up a gravel path to the front door; pressing the doorbell, he waited. Soon, the butler appeared.

"Captain Weiss? Good afternoon. The madam awaits you."

Upon entering, Weiss let his eyes adjust to the penumbra that prevailed inside. The butler led him through a broad doorway and into a salon. Weiss immediately saw her, at the back of the room, sitting before a huge canvas on an easel. She dropped her brush, and went over to him, taking his hand and not letting go. She watched him gaze around the room, which turned out to be a gallery of paintings—all of a considerable size and strewn haphazardly against the walls—each one depicting the phantasmagoric images of a concentration camp. Each painting had a surreal quality as well, for each one included very realistic renderings of forest animals in the background, and sometimes at the edges of the foreground, peeking out, frightened, from the ceilings, and rooftops, or the branches of dead trees.

The large canvas poised on the easel showed a young woman and a man with no face, the latter in the blue-and-white striped pajamas that concentration-camp prisoners wore, and holding a cudgel in his hand. Before this pair, a gang of German soldiers loomed, their faces contorted and grotesque in comparison to the soft featureless face of the man who defended her. The girl bore an uncanny resemblance to Olga. And this face, now, filled Weiss with familiarity.

"Ekdesh!" he muttered.

Olga looked at him.

"Ekdesh. What a lovely word, right? My grandfather also liked it. At times he would become almost catatonic. Ekdesh, ekdesh, he would say. It means butterfly, in Yiddish."

"Butterfly?" asked Weiss, raising an eyebrow.

"That's what my grandfather told me. Where do you know it from?"

"A dream I can't shake."

Olga went over to another painting that showed the same faceless man and pointed at him.

"You sound like my mother. I remember, she used to hear it in her dreams."

"Is that why you paint—to deal with bad dreams?"

She shrugged. "This faceless man used to say it too. Ekdesh. Or at least, that's what my mother said.

"Do you know who he is?"

"No, that's what my mom called him, the man with no face. Her protector. Look, here they are, both of them."

Holding hands, they got close to the picture. Weiss pointed to the figure of the girl.

"It looks like a self-portrait," he said, wondering.

"I look a lot like my mother. That's what my grandfather used to say. And it's true. I can see it in her photos of when she was my age, in Buenos Aires."

"Did she talk to you about the camp?"

"Only about the man with no face. And for some reason, it's what I now paint."

Weiss paused before this image, feeling feverish. He remembered, clearly now, the concentration camp, watching with terror as the arm of a man with a scorpion on it pulled him away from his parents, pushing them in another direction. The face of the hanged man in the boarding house flashed in the captain's mind. Olga's grandfather. Ekdesh.

"I was in that camp, too. As a boy," he said, finally.

"You?" she said, astonished...

"Yes, and I remember her perfectly. You are her spitting image. When I saw you in the morgue I thought you were your mother."

"And my grandfather, do you remember him?"

Weiss didn't have the heart to tell her the truth that he had just confirmed, and he said in a whisper:

"Your grandfather? No... yes... a good man."

Olga could not contain a sob, and she added:

"I saw the news last night. Is it true that my grandfather left a note?"

"Yes," answered Weiss.

"And that ex-captain of the Gestapo? Do you know who he is yet?" she asked, staring at the faceless man in the picture she was painting.

"We have a good lead," said Weiss.

"Remember your promise, Simón," she said, looking him straight in the eyes.

"I haven't forgotten it," he replied, deep in thought. "You can rest assured the murderer won't get away with it," he added. At the same time, Kroneg's figure loomed in his mind.

Weiss pressed her gently toward an open space behind some paintings. He raised her skirt and they made love surrounded by those pictures of horror, seeking an escape from their own fears. Their mutual desire demanded not just joining their bodies but also sharing their dreams.

Some time later, though Weiss could not have said whether an hour or a minute had passed, voices interrupted them. It was Pomerov, just arrived and speaking with the butler. When Pomerov entered, Weiss and Olga were apart. As soon as she saw her husband she ran in his direction. It seemed like she was going to run into his arms, but on closing the distance between them, slipped past him and left the studio. Pomerov saw her go by and then turned toward Weiss.

"It's not the first time," he said.

His voice did not reveal annoyance, not even sadness.

"What's not the first time?" asked Weiss.

"You want to pretend? Then pretend. Did she say anything about her father?"

"No. Was he also in the concentration camp?" said Weiss.

"Olga's grandfather became a kapo to protect his daughter. He protected her from everyone. Everyone, except one man."

"Who?" asked Weiss, as if he suspected what the answer would be.

"A Gestapo officer. Before committing suicide, Olga's mother told her that the Nazi was her father."

Weiss paled and, with Pomerov's words flogging his mind, backed toward the door.

"Her grandfather denied it, but it left a deep mark on Olga. It's her worst torment. Look at these paintings. All she paints is horror," added Pomerov.

"Did you say her mother committed suicide?" asked Weiss.

"She jumped out of a window. Olga was scarcely eight years old. She saw her fall."

"Eight years old," murmured the detective, his face as white as a sheet. He was overcome by a feeling of helplessness, in the face of this absurdity.

"Eight years old," he repeated, his voice trembling, to himself. He had been the same age when he witnessed the death of his parents in the Sachsenhausen camp.

Dragging the weight of his pain for both that little girl and that of his own memories, he headed toward the exit, looking lost. The butler stood there impassively, holding the door. Weiss was about to leave, when Pomerov's voice boomed imperiously behind him:

"Captain, don't allow yourself any hope. None."

The butler closed the door and disappeared inside. Still standing in his wife's studio, a room that dominated not just their house, but their lives, Pomerov cast a glance at his wife's paintings and shivered. A spark of terror burned and died in his eyes.

Weiss opened the door with his key, entered, crossed the lounge bar, and went straight to Margarita's room. Leopoldo watched him pass, perplexed. Margarita, standing, elegantly dressed, watched television. She had switched from macabre footage of the earthquake to a soap opera, and she let herself wallow in its histrionics.

"I've been calling and calling you all night and again all day today. Where have you been?" she said, still staring at the television.

Weiss covered his face.

"Simón, what's the matter? What is it?" she said again.

Weiss took her abruptly by the shoulders and looked in her eyes.

"Margarita, you know how much I love you," he said, stammering. "And that I'd never do anything on purpose to hurt you."

Seized with a chill, Margarita said yes with her eyes.

"And that we've always been honest with each other."

"For God's sake, enough mystery already. Just say it," she said with alarm.

"Margarita, I'm madly in love with you, you know that."

"But," her voice lowered in warning.

"But what's happened is that I've met someone else. Someone whose connection to me is deeper than anything I can control."

Margarita slapped him and immediately embraced him, moaning desolately. Then she stepped back from Weiss.

"Who? Who is she?" she implored.

"No one you know. I just met her yesterday," he said.

Margarita's voice tried to be neutral, but it gave away her pain.

"Yesterday? Then it was love at first sight, like with us."

"Like I said," said Weiss, lowering his head, "It's something beyond either one of us."

Margarita felt like her head had turned into a hornet's nest.

"Who is she? What's her name?" she demanded, grief stricken.

"Olga. A girl."

Weiss's words caught Margarita looking at herself in the mirror, studying her appearance, thinking about the relentless passing of time.

"A girl? What do you mean a girl?" she asked, covering her face.

"Margarita, your public awaits you," shouted Leopoldo from the other side of the door.

As if mimicking the movements of an automaton, Margarita went through her final motions, dried a tear, and applied a bit of rouge. Her lips outlined a bitter grimace.

"Coming!" she shouted, all the grief spilling with that one voice.

Margarita left the room, followed by Weiss, who had grabbed his guitar. The television screen showed scenes of the earthquake, again, as if the soap opera could not block the devastation from coming through for very long. The announcer's voice whispered:

"In several sectors of the capital many buildings and homes continue to collapse..."

Margarita entered the lounge and went straight to the microphone. She was welcomed by the audience's applause, an applause that she couldn't register. Weiss sat on a stool. Leopoldo sat down at the drums. Weiss waited for her to tell him what she was going to sing, but Margarita's mind was a fog. Suddenly, a voice arose from the back of the room. It belonged to one of the prostitutes.

"Margarita, sing 'Blind Love,'" she requested.

There was a brief silence. Margarita remained lost in thought. Weiss and Leopoldo started playing, and then, with a shaky voice, Margarita sang:

"No, don't leave me all alone,
You know I'll die if I'm not with you.
No, don't abandon me,
Today I need you much, much more.
Come to me, for I promise not
To look into your eyes or kiss your lips.
You will give consolation
To this love so blind like my love for you."

Margarita's voice cut off, and she ran to her room. Leopoldo ran after his sister, casting Weiss a withering glance. Weiss lowered his eyes.

———————

Underneath a plate-metal sky, Weiss's car entered the Barranco district, located at about seventy meters above sea level, some twenty minutes from the Plaza de Armas, and which, according to legend, had its origin in the miraculous appearance of a luminous cross on the cliff that had saved a group of fishermen during the foggy season, guiding them safely to shore. After a short drive along a street lined with old European-style mansions with Gothic and Moorish motifs, the car entered an avenue that, cutting through a hill, dropped toward the sea. It then drove around a small square packed with tall trees and bushes, and an enormous house appeared. Set beneath the tall cliffs of the sea wall, the house was on a lane whose sidewalks were partly covered by enormous rocks that had rolled down the precipice. It was protected by a thick stone wall and heavy iron grillwork, through which one could appreciate an immense and beautiful garden, adorned with leafy trees and lovely bougainvilleas that climbed up the mansion's walls. A long path, flanked by classically inspired statues, led to the main door.

The car stopped in front of the gate. Lieutenant Kanashiro got out of the car and walked to the intercom, embedded in the stone wall's right column. He pressed the button.

"Yes?" asked a voice.

"Police. Mr. Müller's expecting us."

"Come in."

The gate opened, and the car entered and parked in front of the mansion's main door. A butler waited for them with the door open. An ex-boxer, with a pair of enormous hands, a pug nose, a network of scars around his eyes, and an unfocused gaze of ice, more than a butler, he looked like a bodyguard. Weiss and Kanashiro went in, and he led them toward the interior of the elegant house. Walking the length of a long hallway, they reached the library. The butler opened the door and bid them to enter. Weiss and Kanashiro went in, scanning the room as they did. Müller received them seated in his armchair, wrapped in his cigar's smoke rings, which played off his silver hair. A Doberman rested at his feet. His gaze was both guarded and defiant, and his bearing suggested that, even at his age, he could move quickly if he wanted, or needed, to.

"Please come in. Take a seat," he said in a mellifluous voice.

Weiss froze, and something inside, the child, cowered momentarily. For a moment, Müller's voice made him that child, again, who, like Olga's mother, witnessed the horror. For a moment, he saw Kroneg—dressed in a Gestapo uniform with pistol pointed at his biological father—dragging his mother into a barracks.

"You don't look well, Captain," Müller said. "Klaus, a cognac. Two—for the officers. Sit down, please."

"We're fine as we are," said Weiss, the anger building inside him, threatening to block out everything but the object of his hate. The butler left the room. The lieutenant kept his eyes on the Doberman.

"How can I help you?" smiled Müller. "My butler mentioned something related to a murder committed in a boarding house."

"Sachsenhausen. Does it mean anything to you?" Weiss took a step forward quickly.

Müller hesitated a fraction of a second.

"Sachsenhausen?" Müller's tongue wet his lips. "I know what I've read about it, which isn't much. Not really my area of interest."

"You arrived in Peru in 1945. Shortly thereafter, you established a business... an important business. Where did you get the money?"

"What could that possibly have to do with a crime in a boarding house?" Müller's voice dripped with sarcasm.

"The victim of that crime was in that concentration camp and left a note that identifies you as the commandant of the Gestapo troops. Sachsenhausen was a concentration camp and the largest Nazi center for counterfeiting bills. More than a billion falsified pounds sterling were found in that camp."

"Don't make me laugh. My name is Johann Müller, and I am a businessman."

"And that's why you had him killed. To keep your new

identity a secret. To hide where your investment capital came from."

Just then, the butler returned carrying a tray with two glasses of cognac. He invited the captain and the lieutenant to serve themselves and both men ignored him.

"Absurd. Absolutely absurd," Müller muttered.

"Maurice Kleimer. What does that name mean to you?" Weiss insisted.

"Not a thing. Who is he?"

"You gave the order to murder him," Weiss accused. Hate boiled in his eyes.

Müller poked the Doberman and the animal stood up on its four feet, opening its cavernous purple jaws. Weiss's image was reflected in the animal's eyes.

"I'm getting tired of your accusations. This conversation is over," Müller said emphatically.

Restrained by Müller, the Doberman got dangerously close to Weiss, who recoiled with fear in his eyes. The animal's jaws, wide open, propelled Weiss into the pool of nightmarish memory. There were too mean dogs at Sachsenhausen, and they all seemed to dislike the people he loved, the people he was imprisoned with.

"Not fond of dogs, Captain? I can't imagine why. Klaus, see them out the door!" shouted Müller.

The butler opened the door for them, and the detectives left the library. As the Doberman settled to its feet, Captain Aránguiz emerged from a side door.

"The Jew's very close with Isaac Montoro," he said.

"And what can they do to me? I had nothing to do with the death of that Jew at the boarding house. Whoever killed him did me a favor."

"At any rate you should still be cautious."

"What do you mean?"

"As for your, let's say, role in the war, you're safe from Peruvian justice, but not from the Israelis. Remember what happened to Eichmann."

"Eichmann was Eichmann. I'm a small fish."

"You should still be careful," recommended Aránguiz.

"Did you see how he looked at me? Why? I don't even know him. But you're right, Captain. It's best to go right to the root of the problem."

"What do you want me to do?" Aránguiz asked.

"Eliminate him. There will be one less Jew in the world."

Aránguiz stood at the window, watching, as Weiss's car crossed through the barred gate and took off down the highway.

Weiss took Kanashiro to his favorite club, located in the Barrios Altos, home of the famous composer Felipe Pinglo. The club was situated on Huanta Street, scarcely a half block from the morgue. The atmosphere was bohemian, filled with smoke that clung to the low ceiling. The captain and the lieutenant were seated at a table on which a pair of empty bottles and an ashtray full of cigarette butts rested. Guttural and deep, the voice of a singer interpreting a waltz reached them:

"Love, being human,
Has something of the divine,
To love is not a crime
For even God loved."

Weiss and Kanashiro had been chatting for a good while. The captain paused, sharply exhaled a puff of smoke, and took a swallow of his drink:

"Kato, your name is identical to the inspector's, except that yours begins with a K. Pure coincidence?"

"I'm named after the inspector, but my father spelled my name with a K to make it seem Japanese. My old man and the inspector are close friends."

"Your old man seems to be friends with everyone."

"There's nothing like friendship," said Kanashiro. "If he taught me anything it's that."

"And do you do honor to your name?"

"How's that, Captain?"

Weiss looked at him, amused.

"Cato, the Roman. 'He's a Cato.' You've never heard that?"

Kanashiro looked at him, not understanding.

"That's said of a man who is just and honest. Are you like that?"

"I try to be, Captain."

Weiss took another gulp. Kanashiro emptied his glass and took the opportunity to ask:

"So, Captain, who was Maurice Kleimer?"

The memory of Kleimer hit him like a knife stab.

"A kapo," answered Weiss.

"A kapo?"

"In the concentration camps that's what they called Jews who collaborated with the Nazis. Some did it to save their own skin, but the majority did it to save their families. That's the way Kleimer saved his pregnant daughter's life—Olga's future mother."

Kanashiro poured himself another drink.

"Captain, your mother also perished in that camp?"

Weiss shut his eyes hard and nodded. Then he took another swallow.

"And Mr. Haas?" asked the lieutenant.

"He's my adoptive father. He saved me from dying in the camp and brought me to Peru. I was ten years old."

"Captain, I've seen films, but I can only imagine the horror of the camps."

"Horror?" exclaimed Weiss, letting out a forced laugh.

"During the war here in Peru the Japanese also suffered a lot," said the lieutenant. "Sure, you can't compare, but the mobs looted the businesses and murdered ten Japanese."

"What the Nazis did to the Jews was genocide," Weiss interrupted him. "And they did the same to the gypsies, for the simple fact of being, of existing."

"Nobody defended us here, Captain. After Japan's attack on Pearl Harbor, Peru deported almost two thousand Japanese to the internment camp at Crystal City, in California. And no one did anything about it. That's why I became a policeman. I wanted to be involved directly with justice, since I didn't get any myself. What about you, Captain?"

"For that same reason. But sometimes the law alone isn't enough to bring about justice."

The owner of the club came over, rubbing his hands and smiling.

"Captain, sing something for us..." he requested.

"In just a moment," Weiss said.

The owner went back to the bar.

"I didn't know you sang, Captain," said Kanashiro. "So your inner artist is in music."

"And yours?"

"If I have one, it would be in drawing," the lieutenant blushed.

"And what do you draw?"

"Faces. Want me to draw you one?"

The captain nodded his head. The lieutenant took out his pen and with quick and sure strokes sketched the face of Olga on the paper tablecloth. Upon seeing the sketch, Weiss quickly poured himself another drink, quaffed it down, and stood up. His gaze was anguished as he looked around the room. "Any requests?"

"A bolero, Captain. 'Crazy Heart.'"

After a brief silence, the captain allowed himself half a smile. He crushed his cigarette and strode to the podium. He shook hands with the guitarist and drummer and whispered in their ears. The few tables in the place grew silent, and Weiss began to sing.

"I can't understand you,
My crazy heart,
I can't understand you, nor can they.
I can't explain to myself
How you can love them both and be so calm
I can't understand how one can love
Two women at once, and not be crazy.
I deserve an explanation
For it's impossible to go on with both of them.
Here goes my explanation,
Since they call me, without cause, crazy heart,
One is a sacred love,
My life's companion,
Wife and mother both at once;
The other is forbidden love,
The complement of my yearnings,
One I won't give up;
And now you know
How it's possible to love
Two women at once, and not be crazy,
And not be crazy, and not be crazy.

SATURDAY, THE 6TH

WEISS WOKE UP anguished and gasping, haunted by the same dream and by not being able to stop thinking about Margarita. He turned on the bedside lamp, and his eyes met a photo of him and Margarita singing. Her fiftieth birthday party. Transported by the song, she looked at Weiss lovingly with glistening eyes. The song came back to him, and then he sang it to himself; suddenly his voice turned into the echo of Margarita's voice, vehement, overflowing, that of a long-suffering woman, treated disdainfully by her lover, and, nonetheless, still in love, convinced—as the bolero's lyrics said—that an old love is neither forgotten nor abandoned, and never says good-bye.

Bathed in sticky sweat, he kissed Margarita on the lips. He returned the photo to its place, lay back down, and closed his eyes, trying to fall asleep again, but he managed only to mire himself in the tangle of his memories. With a growing unease, he opened his eyes again and scanned the room. Nothing was familiar to him. The pictures on the walls, the books strewn everywhere, his guitar resting next to the bed: they all had a different, bleak aspect to them.

Giving the photo a last look, he got out of bed and went to the phone. He held the receiver anxiously, waiting for her to answer. When she did, he blurted: "Let's go for a drive. What would you like to see?"

"Your Lima, Simón," Olga answered. "So that afterwards I can hold onto your memories forever."

"Afterwards?" he said, surprised.

"Yes, afterwards."

"Afterwards when?" But he knew what she meant. He understood completely.

"Afterwards. Stop interrogating me, Captain."

"OK. I'll pick you up in an hour."

"I'll be waiting for you."

Weiss hung up, quickly showered and got dressed. Just then, the phone rang. He went back and picked up the receiver.

"Simón," said Montoro. "You can't touch Müller. Orders from above, from the highest levels. In this case my hands are tied. It's a matter of national security. Do not bother him again."

"Of course, Peru needs weapons," said Weiss bitterly.

"And I'm guessing I shouldn't pass the information to the Israelis either?"

A confirming silence from Montoro.

"Simón," Montoro said hurriedly, "Some things are not worth it."

"Why did you give me the information in the first place?"

"Because I thought I could trust you."

Without answering, Weiss hung up and left his apartment. He exited the building and went to his car, parked just a few yards from the front door. He took Avenida Wilson, recently re-christened by the military government as Avenida Inca Garcilaso de la Vega. The drive was tough. The car advanced by dodging both debris caused by the earthquake and people waving posters featuring the images of the leading Peruvian soccer players—Nene Cubillas, Challe, Cholo Sotil, Gallardo, Perico León, and the captain Chumpitaz. The fans had taken to the streets ahead of Peru's next World Cup match. In their revelry, they tried to exorcize their sorrow and their anger about the earthquake, cheering on the Peruvian team in Mexico, at the top of their lungs, "Peru! Peru! Peru!"

Olga waited for the captain at the door of her house. From her neck there hung a camera. Upon seeing the captain's car, she ran to meet him. From a second-story window, Pomerov watched her, an anxious flame flickering in his eyes.

Simón Weiss's Lima was quite small, a city within a city: Downtown—where he had lived since he arrived there as a child—the Barrios Altos and the Rímac. That Lima included other places that were of vital importance to the captain: the Jewish school in Breña; the brothel where he met Margarita in Jesús María, and, in La Perla, the military academy, whose high yellow walls began to emerge above the Coastal Highway, scarcely twenty yards from the cliff that dropped off to the sea behind a constant veil of fog.

"That's the Leoncio Prado, a military academy. I was a cadet there for three years, from age thirteen to sixteen."

Weiss stopped his car in front of the large barred gate of the school's entrance, guarded by two soldiers.

"Do you want to go in?" he asked.

"It looks like a jail. What happens if later they don't let us leave? I'd rather not," she answered, visibly shrinking from the building.

Weiss turned the car around and headed back towards Downtown.

"Take me to where we met," she said.

"To the morgue?"

"Yes, that area. I want to see what the earthquake has left."

"You're going to see a country that is always falling to pieces."

"Then you're like me, you live surrounded by rubble."

The streets were empty. All of Lima had halted to watch or listen to Peru-Morocco. The spectators' shouts were the only thing that occasionally broke the city's sepulchral silence.

Olga clicked the shutter on her camera repeatedly, and changed her film. She could not help herself; she took pictures of everything, it seemed, every collapsed house and every street full of stones, bricks, and mud. It was the sixth day after the earthquake, and still the devastation was visible everywhere. It looked like the city had been demolished by bombs or flattened by tanks.

"Why so many photos?" he asked.

"They're for my paintings."

He gazed at the young woman. She was drawn to horror, implacably, irredeemably. At San Martín Square Weiss suddenly stopped the car. The first half of the match was over—Peru and Morocco tied at zero—and the square was flooded with drunks who chanted their desperation for a Peruvian victory. A gang of children and teenagers—the notorious Ravens of Lima—had stripped an old man in the middle of the street, leaving him completely naked. Weiss gestured toward the spectacle, cigarette smoke shooting from his nostrils.

"That's my Lima too," he smiled sincerely at the young girl, then leaned over to kiss her. "Stay in the car," he whispered.

Without another word, Weiss got out, slammed the

door shut, and strolled coolly toward the gang. He waded directly into the boys, reaching the old man and shielding him with his body.

"Police. Move. On your way," Weiss ordered calmly, showing them his badge. "And drop the clothes."

The boys waivered, poised to attack him regardless of what he said. Weiss opened his jacket a bit, so that they got a glimpse of the gun holstered under his arm.

"I said move."

They dropped the old man's clothes and backed off, except the leader, a boy of about thirteen, lanky and freckled, who pulled out a switchblade with a sparkling red grip. The other boys whooped as their victim seized the chance to take off down the street, sliding into his pants as he went. Weiss scoffed. The boy lunged. With one swift motion Weiss disarmed him. The boy retreated, glaring at him with hate.

"Son-of-a-bitch! Give me my blade back!" he shouted.

Weiss went at him, his vision paling with anger, and grabbed the boy by his shirt collar.

"Play with blades all you want, but watch what you call me."

The madness in the cop's eyes finally frightened the boy, who went limp in his grasp. For a moment, Weiss lost himself. He pulled the boy down on his knees and shut his fist. Then a voice distant at first, but drawing nearer, stopped him before he struck. It was Olga, standing there amid the boys, like an older sister.

Weiss put the switchblade in his coat pocket and walked through the group, taking Olga's hand as he went. The vehicle started off. Olga trembled in silence. Half a block along, Weiss pointed. At the intersection, a pack of dogs rummaged through overflowing trash, chasing after rats with teeth bared.

"My Lima," he said.

"It feels like rats have taken over everything. They screech all night long. They can drive you crazy," she said, still trembling.

As if in answer to their complaints, from the houses and the bars and the restaurants a swarm of voices exploded. Fans rushed out into the streets, crying *goooal!*

"Let's go to my place," he said. Weiss drove in silence while Olga pointed the camera at herself, taking self-portraits. Soon after, they were making love. He covered her with his body, embracing her greedily, and she submitted to him with her gaze resting on the photo of Weiss and Margarita. The telephone rang. Weiss cast a withering glance at it, but didn't answer, instead turning the young woman's face toward him. They looked at each other intensely, as if trying to discover in the other's eyes some explanation for life's inexorable designs. They knew that they were each made of coincidences and that to love each other was to give their lives over, totally, to random chance.

The phone rang again. Groaning, Weiss slipped out of

bed and picked up the receiver. It was Margarita, who remained silent, trying to rein in her galloping heart.

"It's you, I can tell," said Weiss.

"She's in there with you," stammered Margarita.

"I can't talk now. I'll come by to see you later," he said.

"I promised myself that I wouldn't call you."

"We'll see each other this evening."

Overcome with grief, Margarita could not contain a sob.

"I won't be here. I don't want to see you," she said and hung up.

A blur invaded his mind. He hung up too. He kept squeezing the receiver, choking off a call from the stabbing memory that was sketched on his face, catching Olga's eye.

"It was her, right? Don't leave her alone, go," she said, her voice imbued with compassion.

The girl stood up as if emerging from a dream, caught in the pain that writhed in Weiss's eyes.

"Let's get dressed, come."

He watched her as she reached for his things first, and handed them over. Then she began to dress herself.

"Hurry. It's getting late, and soon the rats will start coming out," she said gently.

As they left they noticed a sharpness in the air, but not the car parked on the corner, whose driver's profile was indistinct from the shadows. It followed, keeping a prudent distance, as Weiss's car took off at full speed down the deserted avenue. The city was still watching the match.

Peru led 2–0 in the closing minutes. The sun was setting. It was a discolored ball above the houses' roofs. Lima's sun, bleary-eyed.

During the return trip Weiss remained silent, and Olga, inhabiting her own world, filled her time by photographing the empty streets at dusk. They finally reached her house, and Weiss stopped the car in front of the half-open door, where Pomerov waited. Weiss looked at Olga with almost paternal affection and she nodded, reaching over to squeeze his hand. They could not help but love each other—this much was clear now. They were the miracle of the life that had endured beyond his parents' murder and her mother's suicide. They existed in the present, two survivors who had come together: that was the miracle.

"Simón, I love your Lima," she said with a smile. "A new city."

Weiss watched her walk away toward her house. He sensed her sadness and loneliness. The miracle could not last.

Upon reaching the door, Olga turned around again and called out toward his open window: "And new cities fascinate me: they're a synonym for adventure."

Weiss started away and after driving a few yards he looked back to contemplate Olga, holding onto her husband tightly. He accelerated along the tree-lined avenue as the setting sun bloodied the ocean, and he felt his doubts and memories clouding his head even as headlights filled the rearview mirror.

Suddenly, tires squealed, and a car pulled up next to him as if out of nowhere. A gun barrel emerged from the darkened window. Two shots fired. Weiss jerked the steering wheel, and his car went up onto the sidewalk and stalled out, with a shudder, just a few inches from a lamppost. Pistol in hand, Weiss leapt out of the car ready to fire back, but the vehicle had already disappeared.

At a phone booth, with a few drunken soccer fans looking on in amazement, Weiss inserted a coin, and dialed a number. With the receiver at his ear, he already had lit his cigarette.

"Hello," answered Montoro. He was in his office.

"Isaac, they tried to kill me. From a moving car. I couldn't see anything. By the time I stopped, the car had disappeared."

"They want to erase you from the picture, Simón," said Montoro. "You played your hand with Kroneg. And if they kill you, you know that nothing will happen to him. You have to be careful."

Montoro hung up. He remained pensive for a few seconds. Then he picked up the receiver and dialed. Weiss hung up also. He had called his friend seeking some answer in his voice, but he'd gotten nothing. Outside, the streets overflowed with people celebrating Peru's qualification for the quarter-finals.

Lieutenant Kanashiro and Sofía were strolling hand in hand when, some twenty yards from her house, a loud screeching of brakes interrupted their conversation. Two men erupted from the car toward the young couple. One of them was Akira Fujimoto, who threw himself at Kanashiro, dealing him a karate chop to the back of the neck that buckled his knees and threw him headlong against the sidewalk. The other man—Nagakata, Tanaka's bodyguard—grabbed Sofía and pushed her toward the vehicle. The neighbors, frightened, did not intervene.

Now Fujimoto was pointing a pistol at Kanashiro. Kanashiro slid his hand toward his shoulder holster, but Fujimoto's voice, speaking in Japanese, stopped him.

"Don't move. The colonel sends you a message. If you want to see her again, take the contents of the safe to the Lotus Flower. Tomorrow at the latest."

Then, still pointing at the lieutenant, he got into the car. In the back seat, Nagakata restrained Sofía, who struggled uselessly.

The car took off as fast and mysteriously as it had appeared.

Kanashiro ran madly toward the street corner, went into the phone booth, picked up the receiver, and dialed. The words came gushing out of his mouth as soon as he heard Weiss's voice.

"Captain, they've taken Sofía. Tanaka's men. One of them was Fujimoto."

Weiss was at Central Police Headquarters. "I can't say it was a surprise but a careless move nonetheless. They must be desperate. Sato," Weiss wondered in a serene voice, as if to himself, "The partner turned rat."

"I couldn't defend her. They took her away before I could do a thing," the lieutenant's voice broke.

"What do they want in return?" Weiss asked.

"The complete contents of the safe, delivered to the Lotus. But Captain, if the secret is out, then why do they care so much about the documents?"

Weiss put his feet up at his desk. "Because photographs matter."

"Surely, they know we'll copy all the documents."

"Things have a way of disappearing," Weiss muttered.

"Aránguiz," Kanashiro deduced.

"Captain," Kanashiro said urgently, "What if we deliver the safe without the documents to the Lotus."

"They'll search us before we get through the door of the Lotus, and they'll make Sofía disappear."

Weiss struck a match slowly and watched the flame tease his fingers before lighting his cigarette.

"What then? We could storm them with a SWAT team."

"Not a good idea. Tanaka is capable of anything and everything, even killing her. We call in reinforcements, and Sofía's life will be even more at risk than it is now."

"Then what do we do, Captain?"

Weiss sighed. "We'll just have to call in other reinforcements."

Leopoldo, who was waiting on some customers, answered the telephone hastily. Margarita happened to be at his side, restocking bottles of gin and pisco on the shelf behind the bar.

"Hello."

"Leopoldo."

"How dare you! You know very well that Margarita doesn't want to talk to you."

Upon hearing her brother's words, Margarita got startled and grabbed the receiver of the extension she had at her side.

"Leopoldo, don't hang up," Weiss hurried.

Margarita felt her breathing cut short by the sound of his voice.

"You really do have a cathedral-sized pair of balls," grumbled Leopoldo.

"Just hear me out," said Weiss. "It's a matter of life and death."

Leopoldo turned to look at his sister, and she, her eyes filling with tears, assented with a glance to the heavens.

"OK, speak," said Leopoldo.

Beneath the dim light of the street lampposts, Leopoldo contemplated Avenida Tacna from the doorway of the Shima Pool Hall. Suddenly Weiss's car emerged from the darkness and pulled to a stop, and the detectives got out of the vehicle. Leopoldo went to meet them.

"Lieutenant Kanashiro... Leopoldo..." Weiss introduced them.

Leopoldo and Kanashiro shook hands.

Weiss drew his weapon, and so did Kanashiro, and the Lieutenant pushed through the newly reconstructed door which swung open easily.

Inside, Tojishiko Sato stood immediately before them, with a shocked expression on his face. With a pencil tucked behind his ears, he carried a cash bag and accounting ledger.

"What's going on?" he demanded, reaching instinctively to shut the door on them.

Weiss forced his way past Sato. With Kanashiro and Leopoldo close behind. Fujimoto, at the back of the pool hall, emerged from a cloud of smoke and rushed towards them.

"You're going to take us inside the brothel," Weiss directed Sato calmly. "Let's go, shall we?"

Sato stepped back quickly, disappearing behind the hulking bodyguard Fujimoto, who spoke quickly in Japanese.

"In Japan he was a champion in karate, in case any of you need a translation," Sato sneered, "And it might be best if you leave before he does something unfortunate."

"Oh really? Tell him I'm the Rímac champion in Peruvian kick boxing," Leopoldo stepped forward, going face to face with Fujimoto and smiling provocatively. "Tell him that I'd love to practice our form together, sometime, in private."

"If I tell him that, he'll kill you right here. He doesn't like faggots."

"Just tell him," Leopoldo egged him on. "Tell him how much I like him."

Sato said something in Japanese and Fujimoto charged Leopoldo. The kickboxer jumped straight up and, while suspended momentarily in the air, used his left foot to deal a sharp kick to his opponent's right ear. Immediately he jumped again and delivered another furious kick with his right foot to Fujimoto's other ear. The body-guard reeled, and Leopoldo finished him off with a head-butt—the cartilage in the big man's nose crackling as his nose was crushed. While Fujimoto crumpled, Weiss grabbed Sato by the neck.

"And now, for our group visit to the Lotus Flower," said the captain.

"Captain, please don't do that to me. If I take you, they'll kill me," Sato implored.

Weiss gave him a shove.

"Then to the roof! Move it! Let's go!"

Weiss forced him to move along with a series of shoves.

Kanashiro and Leopoldo did the same with Fujimoto, who teetered forward, his face painted in blood. They took the stairs, walked up six flights with Sato complaining the whole way, and emerged onto the roof. Weiss and Leopoldo pushed Sato toward the edge of the building while Kanashiro held a pistol to Fujimoto's head. Leopoldo grabbed Sato by the legs and held him dangling over the abyss.

"Don't let go of me! This is an outrage! I'm going to report this!" Sato howled.

"You'll file that report from hell," said Weiss.

"Please, no!"

"Drop him. I want to see his brains make a pretty pattern on the pavement."

"No, no, wait!"

Leopoldo pulled Sato back onto the roof. He held him by the lapels and looked him in the eyes and said, in a whisper: "So now then, who's the faggot?"

Escorted by Sato and Fujimoto, Weiss and his men entered the Lotus Flower without awakening suspicions. Leopoldo went behind Fujimoto, watching him very closely. Crossing the garden courtyard, they went inside, where tall mirrors placed at random reflected the emporium's chief activity: prostitutes, dressed as geishas, attending to their clients' every whim with gracefully artificial gestures.

They reached Kengo Tanaka's office, and Sato knocked on the door. When it opened, Leopoldo gave him a powerful shove and he stumbled inside. Behind a large desk, the fat boss dropped the bundles of cash he had been stuffing in a safe. Tanaka's bodyguard tried to attack, but Leopoldo met him with a drop kick to the temple and they entered the boss's office without anyone from the outside noticing a disturbance. Taking advantage of the distraction and belying his corpulence, a surprisingly agile Tanaka jumped up, a pistol in his hand. Kanashiro, though, was on him like a cat. He landed a sharp blow to Tanaka's forearm, and Tanaka dropped his weapon. Leopoldo subdued Nagakata, pointing a pistol at him. Weiss contained Sato and Fujimoto with his own gun, and they remained motionless. Colonel Tanaka's eyes widened, as he noticed that the police weapons wore silencers.

Kanashiro pressed the barrel of the silencer to the colonel's head while Weiss walked over and examined the bills curiously. He was calm, exceptionally calm. How could it be that the only time that he was truly at peace was when he was floating in the midst of extreme violence?

"I want to see Ms. Galindo," he said. "Call whoever you have to call to bring her in. And careful what you say. If you alert anybody outside, we won't stop shooting until there's nothing left to shoot at."

"She's not here," Tanaka sneered. "You're fucked. The

only way you'll leave this place is feet first. Silencers or not."

"Order them to bring Sofía right now," said the lieutenant. Then he pressed the barrel of the silencer against the colonel's head.

Tanaka picked up the receiver.

"Rita, bring the reporter to my office," he ordered.

He hung up the receiver and looked at Kanashiro.

"You just dug your own grave," said Tanaka to the lieutenant.

"Shut the fuck up!" hissed the lieutenant. Then he said to Nagakata:

"You are going to open the door. Nothing special is going on here, understood?"

Within a minute there was a soft knock on the door. Sheltered behind a wall, Kanashiro signaled the bodyguard to open the door. Nagakata obeyed, and Sofía, dressed as a geisha, stumbled in, a blank expression on her face. Kanashiro pushed Tanaka. "Sit and don't move a muscle!"

Tanaka sat down. Kanashiro kept pointing his pistol at him, but now he was looking at Sofía.

"Darling, come... come close," said the lieutenant.

The girl took some uncertain steps toward Kanashiro. The lieutenant caressed her cheek.

"Sofía, it's me, Kato. What have they done to you? Are you all right?"

The girl lowered her head.

"Honey, answer me. Are you OK?"

Sofía did not answer.

Kanashiro pressed the gun barrel harder against the colonel's head and exclaimed: "What have they done to you? Tell me!"

Sofía hid her face. Kanashiro pressed the silencer against Tanaka's forehead even more forcefully.

"Tell me what they did to you," the lieutenant insisted.

Becoming aware of the situation, Sofía reacted with alarm and tried to push away his weapon.

"Kato... Please, let it go..." she begged.

"Look into my eyes," asked the lieutenant. "Tell me they didn't do anything to you."

Sofía, her eyes filled with tears, could not look at him. She began to cry inconsolably, and rested her head on the lieutenant's chest. He pressed the silencer with still more force. Tanaka looked at Kanashiro with terror reflected in his toad-like eyes. He pointed to the bills piled on the desk.

"Is it money you want? Here it is. It's yours. Take it."

Kanashiro directed his gaze toward Weiss. The captain responded with a subtle movement of his head, letting the lieutenant know that the decision was his. Kanashiro looked at Sofía and, with his eyes glued to the girl, pulled the trigger. Tanaka's body flew backwards, his legs airborne, exposing the little scorpion tattooed on his left calf.

Kanashiro embraced Sofía. At this point, taking advantage of the commotion, Fujimoto lunged sideways and, upon touching ground, rushed Weiss. The captain anticipated the leg coming down on his neck and quickly rolled over and fired before Fujimoto could tackle him. The impact of the bullet threw Fujimoto against the wall. Blood came streaming out from him. Nagakata broke loose from Leopoldo, and the bartender hit him with another frontal head butt. Nagakata collapsed like a rag doll. Sato seized Tanaka's pistol and pointed it at Weiss. Leopoldo, as he was finishing off the bodyguard, managed to spot Sato out of the corner of his eye and, pushing Weiss out of the way, shot him.

"I owe you another one," he said.

"You owe this one to Margarita," Leopoldo replied.

Weiss realized that Leopoldo was wounded in one arm.

"That needs attention," he said.

"It's just a scratch," said Leopoldo.

Kanashiro supported Sofía, who was now more awake because of the shoot-out.

"And now how do we get out of here? This brothel is a fortress," said Leopoldo.

Weiss looked at Sato's body and gestured toward Sofía.

"Kato, dress her in Sato's clothes. Don't forget the hat."

Wasting no time, Kanashiro helped Sofía change clothes and, after moistening his handkerchief with saliva, he cleaned her face of makeup. Weiss had pressed his ear to the door. Leopoldo noticed the mounds of bills on top of the desk.

"What about the cash?" he asked.

Weiss looked at the desk. He walked over to the bills that Tanaka had dropped. Quickly, with his foot he scattered them around the floor and then, gesturing to the wads of bills on top of the desk, he said:

"If you want, take this batch, but leave what's on the floor."

Leopoldo grabbed a briefcase and filled it with bills. Sofía was now disguised in Sato's clothes. Kato covered her head with the hat. Weiss opened the door and peered down the hallway. They went out.

"Let's go out the way we came in," said Weiss when they reached the end of the hallway.

They crossed back through the garden. Through the large windows they could see the brothel's interior, filled with geishas and clients. One guard watched the garden.

"Don't worry. He hasn't seen or heard anything," Weiss reassured them.

When they reached the exit, the guard's back was turned to them.

"Sofía, as you leave, wave good-bye to him," said Weiss.

They passed by the guard without giving the impression that they were fleeing. The guard waved good-bye back at them. On the way to the car, parked some twenty yards from the brothel, Weiss and Kanashiro turned around a couple of times to see if they were being followed. They got into the vehicle. Leopoldo took the front seat, and Kanashiro and Sofía sat in the back. He had his arm around her, comforting her. Tears were running down her cheeks.

"Kato, I'm so sorry..." she stammered.

"Silly, you haven't done anything wrong. You're alive and you are my life," said Kanashiro.

"Kato, remember: not one word to the inspector about what happened," warned the captain.

SUNDAY, THE 7TH

THE SUN WAS setting behind Lima's chronic fog, and a strong wind buffeted the trees. Weiss rang the bell at Olga's house. No answer, so he looked inside through a window. The house lay in darkness and seemed to be empty.

Disappointed, Weiss headed back to his car, when the door opened, and behind him the butler's voice sounded.

"Captain."

Just by looking at him, Weiss sensed that something had changed irreversibly. He returned to the door.

"The madam is gone," said the butler.

"Gone?" said Weiss.

"On a trip. Last night. With her husband."

The butler handed him an envelope.

"This is for you," he said.

Weiss took the envelope and backed away toward his car. He stopped, looked at the envelope, tore it open, took a piece of paper out, and read in silence. He felt that he was being punched in the gut, that an iron fist was crushing his soul. He walked toward his car while reading the letter. The note said:

"*Simón, I write these lines accompanied by my paintings; my ghosts, as I call them. A circle of fire surrounds me, and unless my face is consumed by the flames, a smile like my mother's will remain etched on it after my death.*"

Weiss's hands trembled. He kept reading:

"*I'm leaving, Simón. My strength is waning, and with it my dreams fade, too. But meanwhile I'm still alive, and I want to tell you I love you.*"

Tears streamed down the captain's cheeks.

"*The sun is setting and I must go. To where? I don't know. I return to the earth naked, as naked as the day I was born. Yours always, Olga.*"

Weiss remembered that she had forewarned him. The girl who had witnessed her mother's suicide was anticipating her own death.

The captain wadded the paper in his fist and fell onto his knees on the garden lawn, his chin sunken to his chest, his eyes glazed. Tears kept running down his face. The butler watched him from the second floor. The wind blew harder against the garden and the house.

Weiss smoked and stared at the little television in his living room. At his side was a small table, and, on top of it, an empty bottle of pisco and an ashtray half-full of cigarette butts. Above the TV a photo of the poet César Vallejo hung on the wall. Next to his bed stood his guitar, and above, on the wall, was a photo of Felipe Pinglo. Next to that was a group photo of the Peruvian soccer team, with a caption that read: OLYMPIC CHAMPIONS, BERLIN, 1936. In reality, Peru had not won the championship. It was true that that team, composed mostly of players of African and Indian descent, had defeated Austria 4 to 2, but the Nazi authorities annulled the game and ordered it to be played over on another date. Peru refused to play a second game and the Austrian team went on to lose the final against Italy. However, for Weiss and the majority of Peruvians, Peru deserved the title of Olympic Champions.

Unshaven, defeated, Weiss held a half-empty bottle of pisco in his hand. The TV screen showed the players on the Peruvian team training for their next match.

"Our boys continue to work hard in preparation for the match against the powerful German squad in a battle for first place in their qualifying group," the announcer said.

On the screen Cubillas warmed up with Perico León. Farther on the pitch, Sotil was talking with Didí, the team's Brazilian trainer. The announcer continued:

"A spirit of optimism prevails amongst the players, and many have expressed confidence in a victory that will continue to give the Peruvian people a reason to hope..."

Weiss took a long swallow of pisco and then even a longer drag from his cigarette.

"Moving on to the police blotter," continued the announcer, "a shootout last night at the notorious Lotus Flower brothel, resulted in four deaths. Owner Toshiro Sakura and three of his bodyguards were found riddled with bullets."

The screen showed the scene of the shootout, while the announcer continued to deliver the news.

"The Callao Police suggest robbery as the motive for the murders, since they found an empty safe in Toshiro Sakura's office, and bills strewn all over the floor, cash the murderers apparently could not take with them. They are also considering the possibility that he was executed by a rival mafia engaged in drug dealing and the slave trafficking of women. At the time of his death, Sakura was under investigation for the murder of Tokayoshi Takashima, proprietor of the Shima Pool Hall, as reported a few days ago. It is reasonable, therefore, to speculate that he was eliminated as a sort of payback, since it is believed that Toshiro Sakura's real name was Kengo Tanaka, an ex-colonel in the Japanese army, convicted in absentia as a war criminal. However, the police have made no statement suggesting such a scenario."

Weiss brought the bottle to his lips. At that moment the telephone rang. The captain lowered the volume on the television and picked up the receiver.

"Captain! What the hell happened?"

It was Castro Castro. Weiss would have preferred the inspector to be in a different mood, but that was not the case. This was the inspector at his best. More of a bear than a fox. A grumbler. And what could he say to him?

"Not sure, Inspector. The news knows more than me. The surest thing is that Tanaka was killed for revenge."

"Who killed him, Weiss?"

"Hard to say. Possibly ex-prisoners of the camp Tanaka commanded, or their offspring. There's no shortage of candidates."

"And how do you plan to find them?"

"Is this my case too, Inspector?"

Castro Castro issued a stream of expletives that ended in yes.

"Right, I'll keep you posted, Inspector."

Weiss could hear Castro Castro sigh heavily. "This is becoming problematic, Captain. A bigger problem than anybody imagined. Bigger than you, Weiss. For once."

The inspector hung up and the captain raised the bottle to his lips before pausing, and lowering it without drinking.

Watched from a corner by a man hiding in the shadows inside his car, Weiss stared at the window that faced the lounge-bar of Margarita's brothel. Abruptly, he tossed the cigarette out his car window and took a good snort of white powder. Parked a half block from Margarita's house, he had been debating for some thirty minutes whether to go see her or to step away from her life for good. But his need to see her proved to be greater than his pride, and so, defeated and hopeless, he got out of his car and walked toward what barely a few days ago had been his home.

He opened the door with his key and walked directly toward the bar, where Margarita was mingling with some customers while Leopoldo was serving them some drinks. Weiss proceeded toward the bar, without taking his eyes off Margarita's face. Upon seeing him drunk and defeated, Margarita drained her glass and sat down at one end of the bar. Unable to hide his hopelessness, Weiss extended his arms in a vain attempt at seizing that woman who seemed to vanish before his eyes. He sat down at the bar, across from her.

"Why are you here?" she asked, with a pained voice. "I know. The girl left you, and now you've come back to your mamita."

Weiss raised his head, stared at her, and saw in the depths of her eyes a man—himself—enveloped in a shadow.

"Too late, Simón. I'm no longer your mamita, nor your woman."

Weiss's head dropped onto his arms, which were resting on the counter. His eyes were two burning slots filled with tears.

"Margarita, don't leave me," he pleaded.

"You gave me no choice but to leave you, Simón."

Weiss brought a hand to his breast and clutched his heart. His eyes, sunken and opaque, displayed the wreckage of a dream destroyed.

"It hurts me, too," she said. "And I feel a deep sorrow. Sorrow for me and sorrow for you and sorrow for us."

A tear rolled down Margarita's cheek.

"But do you know who I feel more sorrow for?"

Weiss raised his eyes and his gaze plunged into Margarita's.

"For the child inside of you."

With such painful memories, she had no more to say, and left him to seek refuge in her room.

In the grip of desperation, Weiss heard the slam of the door that shut on him forever. He tried to follow her, but Leopoldo stopped him with a large hand splayed across the bar. He was breathing in heaves and in heaves he begged Margarita not to leave him. He struggled with Leopoldo, but he could not overcome the barman's strength. Leopoldo took him by the shoulders, spun him around, and pushed him toward the exit. Then he threw him out into the street and slammed the door. Lost on the outside and the inside, Weiss looked down both ends of the street, and then walked toward his car, completely drained, trying not to cry out in desperation.

He got in and sped away. Margarita's house, which had also been his house, remained behind like a distant weight, like a weight that increased in proportion to the car's distance from it. He did not notice that the car from which he was being watched was following him, and that behind that car was another vehicle.

After a drive of some fifteen minutes toward the sea, Weiss stopped dangerously close to the cliff edge. The captain got out of the vehicle and drew close to the precipice, leaning forward as if attracted by the void. In front of him the sea extended in all its immensity, and the waves broke against the shore just as he felt his anguish beat against his chest. Along the whole length of the coastal highway, cordoned off by the police to prevent vehicular traffic, one could see the destruction wrought by the earthquake. And as if detaching itself from the highway, like a fan, the city opened, reddened by the setting sun.

Weiss did not hear the engine of the car that parked behind the bushes, some thirty yards from the precipice. The captain had drawn even closer to the rim of the abyss. He needed to breathe fresh air, but it reached him thinned by the memory of the past few days. Events spun in his head. He felt dizzy. His malaise stemmed from an infinite pain, a pain that bore a double face. He thought of Margarita, and he knew her leaving would cost him dearly.

Then his thoughts slipped toward Olga, and his sense of impotence grew in the face of tragic fate, absurd randomness, stupid and irremediable acts. He remembered the girl's parting words: "I'm leaving, Simón. My strength is waning," and then those of Margarita: "You gave me no other choice but to leave you, Simón."

It was not a good night for memories. With his soul swinging between the cliff and the void, Weiss contemplated the familiarity of the city, unchanged despite the earthquake. He thought he recognized the part of Lima his life had revolved around as in a dream. And now, involuntarily, his mind wandered through the streets, the straight and narrow streets that always brought him to the same point, to The House of Thirteen Doors, the home of his childhood, the home of his adoptive parents, the house with the hanged man dangling from its rafters. Kroneg's words echoed in his mind: "And what could that possibly have to do with a crime in a boarding house?"

"Maurice Kleimer. What does that name mean to you?"

And again Kroneg's: "Not a thing. Who is he?"

Then Weiss had a thought that made him shiver: "If not Kroneg, who?" To see through the eyes of others, to see what they saw. That is what the captain wanted.

Lost in his thoughts, Weiss did not notice the man who, hiding in the shadows and the bushes, pointed a pistol at him. Suddenly a shot rang out. Weiss turned around, pulling out his weapon, and saw the man collapsing, getting off a few shots into the air as he fell. The captain spotted another man with a rifle in his hand, one who leapt into a car and drove off at full speed. Weiss ran over to the fallen body. He turned it over: it was Aránguiz. Weiss put away his gun, ran to his car, got in, and sped away.

One lone thought kept tormenting the captain. He understood, all of a sudden, that what separated some men from others is that some wanted to know what they didn't know, and others didn't want to know what they already knew. He felt drained of all emotion, except for a desire for vengeance. Nothing seemed to make sense, except bringing the Kroneg case to an end, whatever that ending might be.

———————

Sheltered by the moonless night, Weiss and Kanashiro climbed over the wall that surrounded Johann Müller's mansion and dropped softly into the garden. Crouching, they moved silently toward the imposing residence. They walked around it and entered through a rear window into a hallway that led to the library. When they reached the door, each pressed his ear to it. The voices of Müller and his butler reached them faintly. At a signal from Weiss, Kanashiro rammed the door open. No sooner had they entered than the Doberman pounced on them like a flash. Weiss's bullet lodged in the dog's heart, and the animal fell to the floor with a whimper.

The butler tried to pull his gun out from his shoulder holster. Kanashiro fired, propelling the man back against the wall, where he then slid, slowly, to the floor. Weiss was pointing at Müller, who tried to stand up, as he was saying:

"This is an outrage! You'll pay for this!"

"Sit and don't move!" Weiss ordered him, shoving him against the armchair.

"What the hell are you doing here?" shouted Müller.

"I've come to look for the butcher of Sachsenhausen," Weiss answered.

Müller regarded him impassively.

"You're a madman. A lunatic. I've already told you that I was never in that camp. I'm not that Kroneg you're looking for. My name is Johann Müller and I'm a businessman."

"Yes, a merchant of death. With these eyes I saw you murder women, children, old men."

"You saw me? What are you talking about?"

"Yes, I saw you murder my father by beating him to death!"

"Your father?"

"And with these very same eyes, I saw you prostitute and strangle my mother."

"Your mother? Who the hell are you?"

"A boy who swore he would kill you."

"I'm innocent. Is it money you want? Name a figure."

"My revenge has no price. I'm avenging a boy."

"Lieutenant, you can't allow..." said Müller.

Kanashiro gave him a look of stone. Weiss' gun barrel was peering into Müller's eyes.

"You're making a mistake. I'm not Gerd Kroneg."

"Get ready to die, you son of a bitch!" shouted Weiss.

"Kill me if you want to, but first I want to make one thing clear. I did not order Kleimer killed."

"So you no longer deny it," answered Weiss. "You are Kroneg."

"Ah, I can see it in your eyes. You know who the killer is. Kleimer wouldn't be the first kapo executed by Jews. Tell me: Do you know anyone who was in that camp? Think hard, Captain. Who else was there?"

Weiss lowered his weapon to relax the tension in his muscles. Müller threw his head back and launched a sinister burst of laughter.

"I knew you wouldn't dare," he said. "You Jews are all cowards."

Weiss raised his pistol again and, with his eyes injected with hate, pointed at Müller's head. A sudden paralysis converted the old Nazi's face into a grotesque mask. Weiss pulled the trigger and Müller's body tumbled backwards. Lips drawn, green eyes flaming, Weiss fired twice more.

"Wait for me outside," he ordered the lieutenant.

Kanashiro looked at him, not understanding.

"I told you to wait for me outside."

Kanashiro obeyed the captain's order, but he left the

door slightly ajar, alert to whatever might happen. Weiss stood at Müller's side and, in a fit of anger, started kicking him furiously.

"You thought you could convince me, you fucking monster!"

Out of control, the captain kept kicking the Nazi's dead body. Suddenly Weiss fell down alongside Müller. Rage and impotence had overpowered him. In his hand appeared a switchblade, the same one he had wrested from the Ravens' gang leader. He used it to cut Müller's pants at his zipper and prepared to mutilate the Nazi's penis and testicles. At that moment, Kanashiro opened the door and walked in.

"Captain!" he said.

Without looking at him, Weiss lowered the knife. He straightened up. He put away the weapon. He went over to the telephone resting on the desk, lifted the receiver, and dialed.

"Isaac."

"Simón. Where are you?" asked Montoro.

"I just killed Kroneg... and his butler..."

"Dammit, Simón. What have you done?" Montoro exclaimed. "I warned you not to mess with Müller. And now? Well, I'll take care of it."

"Aránguiz is dead too. He tried to kill me, but somebody shot him in the back."

"I know. They will find his body next to the Nazi's body.

Simón, what you must do now is get yourself to the boarding house. Your mother called a little while ago. Your old man has shut himself up in the library. It looks like he's got a gun."

Weiss slammed the receiver down onto the phone's base and took off running. Kanashiro followed him.

———————

While the car flew along the highway as if fueled by Weiss's desperation, the captain mulled over words his father had said to him when, as a boy, he revealed he wanted to be a policeman. His father had responded: "Reality writes itself each day, and the important thing for a detective is to know how to read it." And just a couple of days ago, his reading of the facts had opened for him a path which, until now, he had refused to take.

Kanashiro held tight to the door handle of the car, as if trying to reduce its speed.

Meanwhile, at the boarding house, Gustaff Haas had shut himself inside the library, barring the door and blocking it with two heavy bookcases, ignoring his wife's pleas. Seated at his desk, he was writing a note. A gun lay at his side. Esther begged him to open the door, not to do anything crazy.

"Please, Gustaff. Your son is on his way, I'm begging you."

Gustaff Haas stood up and passed the note beneath the

door. Esther the Pole picked it up.

Now Weiss's car sped along a downtown avenue. At that hour of the night the traffic was almost non-existent. Some military vehicles patrolled the city. Weiss increased the speed, and soon the car pulled up in front of the boarding house. Weiss and Kanashiro hit the ground running. They went directly into the boarding house, and when they reached the hallway they heard a shot that shook the doors and windows of the old mansion. The captain and the lieutenant tried to force the door, but it resisted their pounding, pushes, and kicks. Tormented, Esther cried, sobbing with grief. Weiss dropped to the floor and saw through the keyhole his adoptive father with his head bowed over the desktop and the gun still grasped in his right hand. His face bore a smile, like a child peacefully sleeping.

Weiss went to his mother and held her. Then she handed him the note Haas had left. Weiss and Kanashiro went out to the patio. The captain read his father's note in silence.

"I, Gustaff Haas, declare myself to be the sole party responsible for the death of Maurice Kleimer. I killed him because Kleimer had collaborated with the murderers of my first wife and my two small children in the concentration camp at Sachsenhausen. I remember with painful clarity the day when, with his help, the Nazi guards took them to the gas chamber. He appeared at our boarding house without warning, pure happenstance. I recognized him immediately. Before deciding

to take my own life I considered turning myself in, but I feel old and tired, and I don't have the strength to face justice."

Weiss crumpled up the letter, and put it in his pocket. Then he opened the heavy door and burst out into the street, stifling a cry.

———————

As in the lyrics to Pinglo's waltz, artificial light faintly illuminated the extended shadows. Weiss and Kanashiro walked toward the Central Market district, which had been invaded during the previous year by street vendors coming in from the provinces. Old, sleepy Lima had begun to disappear. Now there were signs everywhere of a Lima that was disorderly, pulsating, and vital. Musicians and mimes, religious and political soapbox orators graced the street corners. Prostitutes and transvestites walked the streets in search of clients. The captain and the lieutenant strode in silence, each one disentangling the events of the past six days. Weiss stopped to light a cigarette.

"I couldn't even tell him that Kroneg is in hell," he said.

The two men kept walking. Their shadows projected onto the buildings.

"Montoro took care of everything. It was his man who shot Aránguiz, and it's Aránguiz who will be found dead in Kroneg's library. You'll be ok."

Kanashiro shook his head.

"You know what, Kato?" Weiss spoke again. "Now I understand the meaning of my dream."

"Your father was a righteous man, Captain. And truly brave," said Kanashiro.

"Well, our work here is done, Kato."

"All that's left to do is submit the report to the inspector, Captain."

"And what are we going to report?"

"Whatever you say, Captain."

Weiss clutched Kanashiro by an arm and pulled him fondly along the street, with an almost brotherly affection.

"I've already spoken to The Fox about the crime at the pool hall and the business with Tanaka. I told him Tanaka was killed by someone seeking vengeance. He seems to have bought it."

"So he linked his death to the prison camp."

"Exactly."

"Captain, what about Kroneg?"

"We know nothing about it. Tell the inspector to speak to Montoro. He'll tell him that Kroneg was knocked off by Israeli agents who were hunting him down, or by his own Nazi comrades over... let's say, matters of money."

"The millions of pounds sterling that Kroneg took out of Sachsenhausen."

"It fits perfectly."

"And Aránguiz?"

Tell him he died along with his boss, the Nazi. And if he

wants more details, tell him to call Montoro."

"Excuse me for mentioning it, Captain, but what about your father?"

"Tell him the truth; that it was a suicide."

"Tell him? Won't we be going together, Captain?"

"My work is done. Now I disappear."

"What do you mean, Captain? I don't understand."

"Just that. Tell The Fox that I've disappeared. And that he shouldn't look for me."

"And what will become of your life, Captain?"

"My life? I don't give less of a shit about my life, Kato." Weiss's gesture revealed a deep weariness.

Almost immediately Weiss extended his hand and fleetingly looking him straight in the eye with affection, said: "Well, the moment has arrived."

Kanashiro shook his hand.

"It has been an honor and a pleasure to work with you, Captain."

"Same here, Lieutenant."

Weiss walked quickly away.

"Until the next one, Captain."

Weiss waved good-bye, without turning around to look at him.

"Captain," called the lieutenant.

Weiss turned halfway around.

"What sign are you?"

"What do you think? Isn't it obvious?"

"I knew it, Captain."

"You too, right?"

"Right, Captain."

"It had to be. Loyal to the end."

"The best of friends."

"And the worst of enemies, too."

Weiss started walking again, thinking that he was free to do anything he wanted, even to disappear. Kanashiro watched him walk away.

He wanted to follow him. What they had said to each other struck him as insufficient, but he stood still, his gaze probing the dark of the night. It occurred to him that he didn't know what else to say.

———————

Weiss took a narrow and tortuous street that flowed into the rarified atmosphere of Chinatown. As he rounded the first corner he began to softly hum the waltz that announced the proximity of that world that was at the same time familiar and strange to him. He stopped in front of The House of Dreams. He sounded the old door's metal knocker. After a short while, a boy opened the door and led him along a corridor to the reception hall. In the gaps between the curtains that veiled the entrance to the adjacent room, he could discern the figure of Mr. Komt. The old man greeted him with a bow. His face sketched the outline of a smile, and Weiss felt comforted, anticipating that state in which, bit by bit, reality would crumble apart for him.

Weiss handed his pistol over to him, and Mr. Komt stored it in a closet. Then he invited Weiss to follow him. Suddenly, Weiss heard within him his own voice, but in another place and another time that seemed terribly distant:

"Her eyes are fiery, they drive me mad;
She loves me and offers frenzy,
In her face of cherub or Nereid
Are divined desires of endless bliss."

At that precise instant, with tears in her eyes, beautiful and lofty, Margarita sang before her public:

"Lost love,
If as they say you're living happily without me,"

She wore a desperate expression that lent a mysterious quality to her face. Meanwhile, Weiss and Mr. Komt entered the room with the cots. The old man led the captain to a cot at the back of the room.

Margarita continued, entranced in her song:

"Live happily, perhaps other kisses may give you the joy
That I could not give you."

While Mr. Komt prepared the pipe for him, Weiss took off his shoes, chanting to himself:

"Divine drug, eternal balm,
Opium and dreams give us life."

Mr. Komt passed him the pipe, and the captain inhaled deeply:

"*I breathe the smoke that bestows grandeur*
And when I dream, I am born anew."

Mr. Komt stood next to the cot.

Margarita kept on singing:

"*Today I'm convinced that you were never mine,*
Nor I yours,
You were not meant for me, nor I for you.
It was all a game, but in the bet I gambled and lost.
You can live in peace,
When we cross paths you needn't say hello.
I'm not hurt, and on my mother's soul I swear
I don't hate you or bear a grudge."

Transported by his song, Weiss seemed to answer her:

"*Lovely women fill my harem*
And surrounded by them, I, almost asleep,
Sipping joys, drinking flattery,
I lie in the arms of a woman."

Mr. Komt folded his hands across his lap, with his eyes focused on Weiss, and said in Chinese:

"Man only sees what he thinks is the truth; he doesn't see truth itself. And the truth is that everything we live is a dream."

Inhabiting another world, Weiss seemed to caress the elder's words in his mind.

Now two couples, frenetically immersed in the dance,

glided to the beat of the melody, wrapped in Margarita's silky voice:

"On the contrary, along with you
I applaud pleasure and love."

Immersed in the song's lyrics, reliving them in her flesh, Margarita plunged into the wellspring of her grief, and, wearing a smile that looked like a grimace of suffering, she sang:

"Long live pleasure!
Long live love!
Now I am free,
I love whoever loves me,
Long live love!"

At that point she could take no more; she withdrew inside herself and started to cry inconsolably. All she could manage then was to find the exit door. She was met by the tenuous light of dawn. At that transitional hour there was not a soul on the street. Before her, one could faintly discern the waters of the Rímac, and, at her back, behind the gray and black mountain peaks, clashing with the mist, the newly born sun projected a pale reflection onto the city. A strange fog fell, thicker and denser than usual, dissolving everything into an unreal vision.

TRANSLATOR'S NOTE

ISAAC GOLDEMBERG FIRST came to my attention when, roughly in 1980, I was doing research to revise my doctoral dissertation, on narrative irony in the contemporary Spanish American novel, as a publishable book. His first novel, *La vida a plazos de don Jacobo Lerner* (translated into English by Robert Picciotto as *The Fragmented Life of Don Jacobo Lerner*), was receiving high praise from book reviewers and literary critics in both the United States and throughout Latin America. I wanted my first book to be broadly representative in studying the avant-garde novels being produced since the Boom period of the 1960s, and *Don Jacobo Lerner* was an excellent text for that purpose. It was ironic in the sense that the meaning of the work cannot be arrived at through a literal, linear reading. The novel features frequent jumps in time and space, such that a chronological plot can only be arrived at in the reader's mind through reconstruction of the elements; and the multiple narrative perspectives, along with numerous inserted documents, create a kaleidoscopic experience. If meaning is to be had (and that is precisely what is at stake), it must be sought in the interplay between the numerous brief texts, many of which are not necessarily in consonance with each other. *Jacobo* remains a playful, tense, and elusive work, one that shares space with the likes of Julio Cortázar, Carlos Fuentes, Gabriel García Márquez, Manuel Puig, Juan Rulfo, and Mario Vargas Llosa.

Goldemberg was already living in New York City at the time, and I was working at Cornell University, in Ithaca, New York. So it was not inconvenient for us to meet, and for me to gain a sense of the man behind the book. The resulting chapter on Goldemberg's work was incorporated into my book on narrative irony, which went on to be published and contributed to my earning tenure and going on to enjoy a long career in academia.

It was not until late 2003 that Goldemberg and I met again. We found ourselves on the same panel, dedicated to his work, in a conference at Brown University. In that session I discussed his other novels, including *El nombre del padre* (*The Name of the Father*), a further elaboration of the lives and times of some of the same characters from *Don Jacobo Lerner*. By filling in many of the gaps created in the first novel, Isaac now created different, more challenging gaps in the narrative constituted by the sum of the two texts.

Since that conference, Goldemberg went on to become Distinguished Professor at Hostos Community College and Director of the Latin American Writers' Institute, and has garnered half a dozen prizes for his writing in both prose and poetry. I myself was invited to become an honorary editor of the journal Goldemberg directs, *Hostos Review/Revista Hostosiana*. And yet it wasn't until 2013, when he sent me a newly published collection of his poetry, that the idea of translating Goldemberg was sparked. I'd taught Spanish-American poetry on numerous occasions, but I had not published a word on the subject, nor had I ever attempted to translate poetry. In reading the poems from *Diálogos conmigo y mis otros* (*Dialogues with Myself and My Others*), however, I found I not only understood what they were saying, I also understood where the poet was coming from in terms of his Peruvian-Jewish worldview, his sense of being exiled in a small boat on a rough sea, his Holocaust-driven demons, his love of language(s), his ambivalences, his wry jokes, his erudition. Something inside me said it was time to face the poetic music.

When I proposed a translation of the collection, Goldemberg's unhesitating response was *luz verde* (green light). Regarding the process of mounting that translation, no author has ever given me so much of his time, effort, and expertise. Fortunately, his English is excellent.

We were therefore able to dialogue intensely about the nuances of terms in both Spanish and English, and even the appropriateness of using a verb like the Yiddishism "to schlep" for the Spanish *arrastrar* in the translation. The translated collection is now complete, and being considered for publication in the US, UK, and New Zealand.

And so we come to the text at hand, a hard-boiled detective novel (*novela negra* in Spanish) that manages to be both a parody of and homage to its archetype. That is, while it conforms to the formulaic conventions of the commercially motivated object, through exaggeration and occasional deviance from those constraints (the character Leopoldo, an Apollo-like gay bartender, who is as courageous as he is strong, stands out in this regard), it also can be construed to wink an eye and self-consciously question its traditional aesthetic limitations. Set in Lima, during six days (suggestively, in biblical terms, a Tuesday through a Sunday; in recent historical terms, the length of an Israeli war) in June 1970, *Remember the Scorpion* features all the melodramatic and kitschy characteristics proper to the hard-boiled genre. A tremendous earthquake has just struck the Peruvian capital, and mayhem reigns throughout the city, but for the World Cup soccer matches, which bring the entire population momentarily back to some sort of mesmerized calm. True to the novel's archetypal, Chandleresque form, the hero is far from perfect, but he is a brilliantly artistic sleuth, and, a passionate man who is not immune to love even in the face of catastrophe.

Linguistically speaking, the novel is careful to avoid becoming overly complicated, employing a narrator whose voice and vocabulary are dialed at approximately the level of journalistic prose. The characters may use some contractions, obscenity, or cops-and-robbers parlance when they speak, but the narrator is steadfastly reportorial. Every so often, however—perhaps once or twice a page—a situation of acute verbal ambiguity comes along, causing the translator to stop and reflect.

Inter-cultural misalignment also plays a role in muddying the translational waters. Weiss, a captain in the Lima police force, is assisted by Lieutenant Kato Kanashiro, a culturally inclusive move, but Goldemberg does not take long to remind us of the times in which the novel is set. Kanashiro is engaged to a "*muchacha*" ("girl") named Sofía Galindo, a locally renowned TV news reporter. Sofía is twenty-five years old and a successful professional in the nation's largest and most important city, but she is consistently still referred to as a muchacha. Although this word sometimes still means a servant or maid, throughout the Spanish-speaking world these days it is primarily understood to mean a less-than-adult female. What's more, her detective fiancé is also called a "boy" (*chico*). It's not that feminist and Left-leaning political movements weren't confronting sexism and racism in the early 1970s; it's that the Culture Wars of the late 80s and 90s had not yet been fought, and language *vis à vis* gender and race operated very differently. And being reminded of the relativity of such factors is not a bad thing.

Language is a living and breathing organism, and to keep pace with its developments it is important for a translator to go beyond dictionaries—through travel, consulting with native-speaker colleagues, surveying chat groups, and watching Telemundo and feature-length films, among other potential sources. A word like *mamita*, for all of its maternal connotations, is also a term of endearment, not unlike "baby," "honey," or "darling." My first impulse was to go with "sweetheart," but that sounded too Humphrey Bogart. Slightly more contemporary would be "sugar babe" or "baby doll." But those sobriquets have also not aged well in the hip-hop era. Ultimately, we decided to leave it as *mamita*, in all its strangeness and familiarity, its semantic suggestiveness and phonic resonance. Sometimes the best translation is no translation at all.

All of this demonstrates that translation is a special kind of writing that entails a prior hyper-reading. Who but a translator gets to dwell undisturbed in inter-lingual and intercultural space for weeks and months on end? It is perhaps because of the bliss embodied in the translational process that the translator's function commands so little respect, as if one were dealing with just another video game junkie. Ah, but then there is the text, the product of so much time spent in "idle play." The materiality of the text (even a virtual one) ensures, through the translator's alchemy, that the source text may now have an audience in an entirely new and different linguistic and cultural zone. Readers of translations, whether hyper-readers or not, have a window onto worlds they could not otherwise access. If, in viewing the world of *Remember the Scorpion*, readers manage to glean some of the almost euphoric joy this exercise awakened in me, the effort will have been entirely worthwhile.

JT

ABOUT THE AUTHOR

ISAAC GOLDEMBERG, born in Peru in 1945, is a renowned poet, playwright, and fiction writer. He has lived in New York since 1964 and is the Distinguished Professor of Humanities at Eugenio María de Hostos Community College of the City University of New York, where he is also the Director of the Latin American Writers Institute and the Editor of *Hostos Review*, an international journal of culture. He is the author of four novels, including the critically acclaimed *Play by Play* and *The Fragmented Life of Don Jacobo Lerner*. He has also published several collections of poems, including *Hombre de paso/Just Passing Through*, *Los autorretratos y las máscaras/Self-Portraits and Masks*, *Los cementerios reales* ("Royal Cemeteries"), *Libro de las transformaciones* ("Book of Transformations"), and *Diálogos conmigo y mis otros* ("Dialogues With Myself and My Others"). He lives in New York.

ABOUT THE TRANSLATOR

JONATHAN TITTLER is a Professor Emeritus of Hispanic Studies with Rutgers University. He has held the Prince of Asturias Chair in Spanish at The University of Auckland, New Zealand, and has chaired the Department of Romance Studies at Cornell University. His credentials in translation include six Spanish-American novels: *Juyungo*, by the Afro-Ecuadorian writer Adalberto Ortiz (Washington, D.C.: Three Continents Press, 1982); *Bazaar of the Idiots*, by the Colombian Gustavo Alvarez Gardeazábal (Pittsburgh: Latin American Literary Review Press, 1989); *Chambacú: Black Slum*, by the Afro-Colombian Manuel Zapata Olivella (Pittsburgh: Latin American Literary Review Press, 1991); *Love – Fifteen*, by the Chilean Antonio Skármeta (Pittsburgh: Latin American Literary Review Press); *Changó, the Biggest Badass*, by the aforementioned Zapata Olivella (Lubbock, TX: Texas Tech University Press, 2010); and *El gato eficaz* (*Deathcats*), by the Argentinean Luisa Valenzuela (Portland, OR: Gobshite Quarterly/ Publications Studio, 2010). *Changó, the Biggest Badass* earned Honorable Mention for the MLA's 2011 Lois Roth Award for the Translation of a Work of Literature.